My Farmhand
A Psychological Thriller Novel

By Keewee Tully

Table of Contents

Chapter 1...1
Chapter 2...13
Chapter 3...19
Chapter 4...32
Chapter 5...37
Chapter 6...51
Chapter 7...61
Chapter 8...67
Chapter 9...75
Chapter 10...82
Chapter 11...88
Chapter 12...98
Chapter 13...106
Chapter 14... 113
Chapter 15...124
Chapter 16...133
Chapter 17...140
Chapter 18...147
Chapter 19...149
Chapter 20...160
Chapter 21...168
Chapter 22...173
Chapter 23...177
Chapter 24...190
Chapter 25...199
Chapter 26...208
Chapter 27...215
Chapter 28...218
Chapter 29...219

Chapter 30 228
Chapter 31 234
Chapter 32 240

---

1. https://www.myidentifiers.com/title_registration?isbn=979-8-9908616-1-9&icon_type=New

2. https://www.myidentifiers.com/title_registration?isbn=979-8-9908616-0-2&icon_type=New

This book is emotional, graphic and controversial
Recommended for ages 18 and up
This book contains:
Graphic violence
Domestic abuse
Sexual situations
Profanity
Adultery
Certain situations may be deemed offensive and triggering

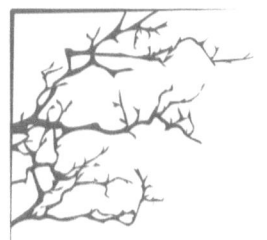

Chapter 1

It was late at night, and I found myself standing over my husband James while he slept. I am holding a big kitchen knife in my hand. The room is dark, but there is moonlight coming through the window, giving off just enough light to see him. He is sound asleep on his back and part way under the blanket. His white tee shirt is almost glowing in the pale moonlight. I watched as his chest moved up and down with every breath. It was so quiet, I could almost hear the beating of his heart.

I knew he needed to die. He has to die. He can't keep hurting people and continue to get away with it. I have to do this for Anthony and I. It's the only way we can be together forever.

I gripped the knife handle tight in my hands and slowly raised my arms above my head. I froze. I told myself, "Come on, you can do it. All you need to do is give it one hard thrust into his throat and it will be over for good. Do it, Cindy, do it." I felt my arms tense up as I tightened my grip on the handle of the knife. I paused, only for a second, to get one last look at his smug face. Then I swung the knife down, almost piercing him, stopping right before it would have plunged deep into his throat. "Oh, shit!" I said. James moved one of his arms and I panicked.

I hid the knife behind my back and scurried out of the room as fast as I could go.

I put the knife back where I got it from in the kitchen and jumped back onto the couch. My heart was pounding and adrenaline was rushing through my body. I couldn't believe myself. I was only a split second away from killing him and I chickened out. I wanted to watch him bleed. I wanted my face smiling at him to be the last thing he saw, and me whispering into his ear, "Goodbye, James" to be the last thing he ever heard.

I woke up gasping for air and struggling to breathe. It was just a nightmare, but it felt so real, like the night I was going to kill my husband. It's almost impossible to catch my breath, and I am covered in sweat, trembling. There is something to the right of me making a constant beeping noise. I don't know where I am or how I got here.

Beep. Beep. Beep. It hurt to open my eyes. My head is pounding with a dull, throbbing pain like I've never felt before. It took a few minutes for me to realize I'm in a hospital room and lying in a bed. Why am I here and how did I get here? There are I.V. lines and tubes running all over the bed. There's also wires attached to my chest and head. When I tried to yell for help, I couldn't. I realized I have a tube down my throat so I started to panic. Everything is a daze, and I am very confused. I tried to sit up, but couldn't. The first thing I did was reach for the tube in my throat to pull it out. A nurse came rushing into the room and stopped me just in time.

"Well, look who's awake. Don't move Cindy, and we can get that out," she said. She slowly pulled on the tube until it was free from my throat. I felt better for the moment, or at least relieved I no longer had something going down my throat. She handed me a small cup of water and a little stick with a sponge on the end. "Here dear, dip this in the water and bite down to wet your throat. I'm sure it's pretty dry," she said. My throat was so sore, I almost couldn't swallow.

That's when the doctor came in to talk to me. "Hi, Cindy, I'm Dr. Smith. Do you know where you are?" I nodded my head up and down. "Do you know why you are here?" he asked.

"No, I don't remember. Why am I here?"

He glanced over at the beeping monitor while writing on his clipboard. "Cindy, you got thrown from a horse and smashed your head on a rock. You suffered a traumatic brain injury and some skull fractures. We had to put you into an induced coma for a week to get the swelling in your brain down. We are concerned about your condition," he said.

I reached up to feel my head, and most of my hair was missing in the back. I could feel a huge bald spot where my hair used to be. The back of my head is also very sore and I could feel staples running across my skull like railroad tracks. I felt horrible and I'm sure I must look the same.

I tried to focus on what the doctor was saying, but I kept drifting in and out of consciousness. His voice sounded so muffled, I couldn't make out what he was saying anymore. It wasn't long before my eyelids were too heavy to hold open. Soon, I fell asleep.

The next time I woke up, I felt like a truck hit me. There is a constant ringing in my head and the headache I have is almost unbearable. I tried to turn my head and look around the room, but my neck was so stiff and sore, I couldn't move.

As I lay here feeling alone, depressed and confused about everything, I looked through the window of my room and I could see it was dark outside, but I was unclear about what time it was. There is a round dial clock hanging on the wall across the room, but I couldn't make out the time. My eyes hurt and my vision is a little blurry, assuming it's from whatever medications I'm on. I didn't know what month or what day of the week it was.

The only thing I could do was lie here and think, and the only thing I could think of is Anthony. I imagined him walking through the door, wrapping his arms around me and telling me everything was going to be okay. I want to smell his scent and feel his warm touch. I need him here with me. The way he makes me feel safe and secure when he is around soothes me. Does he know where I am? He must. Has he come to visit me? I'm sure he has. Why wouldn't he? He loves me and wouldn't just abandon me. I don't want to think about it, it's too depressing. The thoughts and questions I have are tearing me apart inside. Here I was, lying in a hospital room, alone and confused.

While on the verge of having a breakdown, I realized I could call him. There has to be a phone in here. I could almost see the side table next to my bed out of the corner of my eye, so I picked up my arm and reached as far as I could. I started feeling around the tabletop and almost knocked off my cup of water the nurse had left there. Then I felt it, that all too familiar phone cord. The kind of coiled cord you can stretch clear across the room. I grabbed it in a hurry.

I have to hear his voice. I have so many questions. He needs to know I miss him and I want to see him. I tried to focus on the buttons while I dialed his number, then I put the phone up to my ear. "The number you dialed is not in service. Please check the number and try again," then a busy signal. What? No, that must be wrong. Did I misdial his number? I panicked and tried again. "The number you dialed is not in service. Please check the number and try again." My heart sank as I started to sob and cry myself back to sleep.

It wasn't long before the nurse came in and woke me up to check on me. I wanted to know what was going on. I looked up at her and asked, "Excuse me, has anyone come to visit me since I've been here?"

"Yes, your husband James came in once and some woman named... Let me think for a minute."

I interrupted her. "Vicky. Was it Vicky?"

"Yes, as a matter of fact, her name was Vicky."

Then I asked her, "Has a guy by the name of Anthony come in to visit me?"

I was overcome with sadness when the nurse said, "No, not that I know of, but I'm pretty sure your husband will be in to see you as soon as he can. Dr. Smith left a message on his phone, letting him know you're awake. So, how are you feeling today? Any symptoms I should know about?" she asked.

"I have a nasty headache, ringing in my head and a sore throat. I am also exhausted," I said.

"That is likely because of your injury and the drugs we have you on. How about your vision? Do you see any flashing or strange lights? Any dark spots or fuzzy floating spots?"

"No," I replied.

She held my eyelids open and waved a penlight at my eyes. "That's good, and your pupils are responding well to light. Try to rest and get as much sleep as you can for now. You need to remember that your brain is still trying to heal itself."

Once she left the room, my thoughts went straight back to Anthony. I missed him so much and I couldn't get him off of my mind. I needed to hear his voice.

I still felt drowsy and I could feel my eyelids getting heavy again when I noticed a faint, dark, manly figure enter the room. I tried to adjust my eyes and focus. As he got closer, I could make out he was wearing a suit and had a thin stature. He walked up to my bedside, and I recognized his familiar voice as he spoke. "Hi Cindy, it's good to see you're awake."

I was disappointed to see it's my husband. "Hi, James."

"Cindy, I'm so sorry I didn't get here sooner. I was on my way back from my trip when I got a message from the doctor that you're awake. As soon as I got it, I rushed right over." He leaned over the bed and gave me a long hug, then kissed me gently on the forehead. "How are you feeling?" he asked.

"Not so great," I said.

He reached down and placed my hand in his. His hands felt soft, dainty, and smooth. They are nothing like Anthony's tough, masculine hands. He looked at me with pity. "I can only imagine how you must feel. You had a terrible accident, but the important thing is you're alive. I was so worried about you."

"James?"

"Yes, Cindy?"

"How did this happen to me?"

He paused for a moment and said, "You were out riding the horse and fell off somehow. Maybe something spooked it? I got home from work late, expecting to find you in bed, but you weren't there, or in the house. I thought it was strange, so I went outside calling for you. I noticed the horse standing near the fence with a saddle on. I went to see what was going on and that's when I found you laying on the ground, unresponsive. Your head was lying on a flat rock and there was blood all over the ground. I thought you were dead. I panicked and called 9-1-1. You are so lucky to be alive. You really don't remember?"

"No, I don't remember anything about my accident. It's frustrating. Anyway, how are things going with you?"

"I've been as good as I can be, you know, with you being in here and all. There's been difficulties. I have been so scared you would never come out of the coma. I can't imagine my life without you. It hasn't been easy. And work? Well, you know how it is. It keeps me busy. Which, for the last week, has been a good way to keep my mind off of what happened. So I guess my job has its benefits."

"James, what about the horses? How are they doing? Are the animals being taken care of?"

"The horses are fine. You have more important things to worry about, such as getting better. Vicky has been going to the house every day to feed and water the animals while I'm at work. She's also been helping me with my laundry and keeping the house in order. She is such a good friend to you. You are so lucky to have her, and I'm also very thankful for her."

My heart started pounding and I'm sure James could notice the panic in my voice when I asked, "Vicky has been taking care of the animals? What happened to Anthony? Did he go back home? Did you fire him? Where is he, James?"

James gave me an odd, strange look and said, "Not this again."

"James, tell me, is Anthony still there? I need to know."

"Cindy, there is no Anthony. How many times do I have to tell you he only exists in your mind?"

"James, you do know him. You hired him to help me around the farm. He was staying with us. You know... Anthony."

He gave me the same strange look he gave me a second ago and said, "There is no Anthony, Cindy. Are you sure you're feeling okay?"

My heart sank, and I almost started crying. I didn't want to come across as crazy to him, so I said, "I don't know. Everything is so confusing to me right now and I don't feel like myself. Maybe I had some strange dream or something?"

He caressed the back of my hand. "You're suffering from a bad brain injury, so I guess anything is possible. Why don't you get some rest and I will come back to see you when you're feeling better? I love you," he said.

James walked out of the room. I could see him standing in the hallway through the big window that separated the hall from my room. Why is he just standing there? Then I saw Dr. Smith walk over and start talking to him. They must have talked for fifteen minutes or more.

I couldn't believe what James said to me. Is he lying, telling me he doesn't know who Anthony is? Anthony was his idea. He hired him. He also asked him to stay with us, and now all of a sudden, he doesn't know who he is? Is my brain injury so bad I am imagining things? Why do I remember everything about my relationship with Anthony as if it were yesterday? If he doesn't exist, then how come I miss him? If he isn't real, then why do I love him so much? Why is this happening to me? James must be lying. Is he trying to hide something? Where is Anthony when I need him and why isn't he here to comfort me? I know he loves me. He told me so on our horseback ride and every day since then. I just want to snuggle my face into his chest and let him hold me.

Once my heart rate fell back down to normal, I fell back to sleep. I didn't sleep through the night. It is pretty impossible to get a full night's sleep when there is a nurse coming in every couple of hours just to make sure I can still wake up. I get why they do it, but it is very annoying, especially with all the silly questions they ask me repeatedly. Questions like, do I know my name or do I know where I am?

The morning came a little too soon for me. My eyes hurt every which way I tried to move them. My head was throbbing worse than yesterday and it was ringing even louder since waking up out of my coma. I reached over and pressed the call button for the nurse. She came into my room right away. I told her how I was feeling and asked for some water. She left, came back a few minutes later, handed me a small bottle of water with a straw and put something into my I.V. for the pain. It didn't take long before I felt numb from the drugs she gave me.

Just when I felt like I was going to drift away into sleep, I saw the door to my room open. The first thing I noticed was bright red lipstick, long shiny dark hair and brown sparkling eyes that brought attention to the pretty face behind it all. As she stepped through the door, the smell of her perfume spread throughout my room. She had on black high heels and a pinstripe power suit. There was no mistaking who it was. Her slender, athletic build gave it away. It was my best friend, Vicky.

I heard her say, "Oh my goodness, sweetie, you're awake." She made her way over to my bed and stood there for a few seconds, looking down at me. She looked like she was struggling to hold back the tears that were forming in her eyes. "It is so good to see my bestie up and alive." She sat on the edge of my bed, leaned down, and smothered me with the warmest hug.

I almost started crying. "It's so good to see you, Vicky. I've missed you."

She looked at me with her brows slanted, pushing out her lower lip as if to sulk. "When James called me and told me you're awake, I wanted to come right over, but as soon as I got back into town, I had to go sign papers on a new health club I'm opening."

"It's okay, Vicky. James came to visit me yesterday when he got into town and he didn't stay long because I was feeling horrible, so don't beat yourself up over it."

Then she turned her head and looked away to avoid eye contact with me. "Oh yeah, that's right, I forgot he was out of town."

"Vicky, can I ask you something without you thinking I'm crazy? I asked James, and he looked at me like I was crazy, but I know I'm not. I can't be."

She grabbed my hand and held it. "Sure sweetie. You ask away."

I looked her right in the eye and asked, "Where is Anthony?"

Vicky raised one brow and turned her eyes up at the ceiling. She looked like she was trying to process what I just asked her, then I got the same puzzled look from her I got from James. "Cindy, sweetie, who is Anthony?" she asked.

I felt a wave of despair wash over me. "Oh no, not you too, Vicky? James said the same thing to me."

"Well hold on, Cindy. Maybe I just don't remember. Tell me who Anthony is and let's try to figure this out together."

"Vicky, you wouldn't have forgotten so soon. He's my farmhand, who I've been seeing for quite some time now. James hired him to help me around the farm, and I told you all about him the last time you came to visit me at home. You promised me you would keep it a secret, and you were proud of me for making myself happy again because you thought James was being an asshole to me."

She gently squeezed my hand. "That sounds like something I would say, but I'm so sorry, Cindy. I don't remember us discussing anything like that. It seems like something I wouldn't forget. Are you sure you're feeling okay?"

Tears started streaming down my face. I said, "I don't know. I'm so confused and I don't know what to think anymore."

She handed me a tissue, then leaned back down and gave me another hug. "Well, you don't worry about those things right now. You've had a horrible accident and you're going through a lot. I'm sure many things are confusing to you now. And don't worry about the house or the animals. I've been taking care of those things for you and I even bought you a shiny new cast-iron skillet to replace yours because I know how much you love that ridiculous pan. I don't know why you like it so much? It's too heavy, and it's difficult to clean. I was considering getting you a nice lightweight Teflon pan like the rest of us normal people use."

"Thank you, Vicky, but what was wrong with my pan?"

She reached out and pushed back the hair from my face. "Sweetie, a few days after they admitted you to the hospital, I found it rusting away in a bucket of nasty water on the back porch. I figured you burned something in it and were soaking it. It was disgusting, and I didn't want to touch it, so I threw it away and got you a new one. You know I love you, but I wasn't ready to break a nail scrubbing the grime off of that thing."

"Thank you, Vicky. I don't remember putting it out there in a bucket."

"Okay, sweetie, I'm going to take off so you can get that brain of yours back to health. I still haven't unpacked my luggage yet. Make sure you get better. I love you, girl. If you need anything, and I mean anything, you call me." She gave me another big hug, and I said, "Okay, love you too."

Then she walked out of my room and stopped to talk to the doctor just as James did, which I found strange. I wish I knew what they were discussing with the doctor.

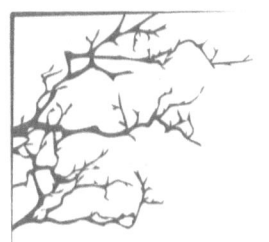

Chapter 2

I couldn't stop thinking about what Vicky said and wondering why she didn't know who Anthony was. I felt like I was falling or drowning. How can James and Vicky not know who Anthony is? Why was my pan in a bucket on the porch rusting away? That is not somewhere I would leave my favorite pan. I always wash it and put it right back on the stovetop. What she said doesn't add up at all. I have too many questions.

I remember the day Vicky came by the house. I heard a knock on the door and went to look out the window. She was standing there, holding a bottle of wine. She yelled at me through the door. "I see you looking through the window. Open the damn door, girl. I brought wine."

I barely got the door opened when she pushed her way in. She tossed her purse onto the counter and turned to look at me.

"What brings you here, Vicky?"

She placed her hand on her hip. "You would know if you answered your damn phone once in a while. I haven't seen you much lately, and I wanted to check on you to make sure you're still alive. James could have killed you and buried you in the basement for all I know. What? Don't look at me like that. Shit like that happens, you know. Have you ever watched those crime shows on television?"

"Vicky, oh my gosh, you're so crazy."

She smiled. "You're now just figuring this out? Come on, Cindy. Let's go sit out back and do the responsible thing."

I looked at her confused and asked, "Responsible thing?"

She raised the wine bottle up in the air and shook it at me. "Yeah.. drink, Cindy. Don't forget to grab a couple glasses and an opener for this bottle," she ordered me. Then she walked through the back door and made her way out to the lounge chairs by the fire pit.

I went out and sat in the chair next to her. She opened the wine and poured our glasses. We talked about how my marriage to James was going and what he was putting me through. I got emotional and almost cried.

Vicky got annoyed and agitated with James. "He's an asshole, Cindy. What kind of man would bring you all the way out here and leave you by yourself all the time? A real asshole, that's who," she said with disgust.

I took a big gulp of wine. "As much as I hate him, James did one thing right," I said.

She looked at me with curiosity. "Oh, really? What did he do?"

I couldn't help but smile big and say, "James hired a farmhand to help me around here. His name is Anthony. He is so dreamy and good with his hands."

With a sarcastic tone in her voice, she responded, "He did? Where is this hunk you speak of?"

I turned my head in both directions, looking around for Anthony. "I don't know. I think he's here somewhere, unless he went to town for something. Was his truck out front when you got here?"

"No, there was no truck in the driveway when I got here," she said.

"Yeah, Vicky, you know what? I bet he ran into town to grab something."

She leaned toward me with a gratifying look on her face and said, "You should let me borrow him for a night. I will show him who is good with their hands."

I couldn't believe what she said to me. As if she doesn't get enough guys in bed already. Don't get me wrong, I love Vicky to death, but she is relentless when it comes to "landing" the next guy. I responded by snapping at her, "Um, no! I don't think so! Get your own guy."

That is when her eyes widened considerably and her mouth fell open, saying, "Oh my gosh, Cindy, I know what's going on here! You're having sex with him! Are the two of you sleeping together?" Her curiosity brought her to the edge of her seat with a look of anticipation on her face.

"Vicky! Why would you ask me that?" I instantly regret opening my big mouth about Anthony. What was I thinking? She will not let this one go. I took another big gulp of my wine.

Her gaze was focused directly on me. "Cindy, look me in the face and tell me you're not having sex with him," she pressed.

She caught me. There was no hiding it now. I couldn't lie to her and I never should have opened my stupid mouth. I rolled my eyes back and let out an enormous sigh.

She blurted out. "I knew it!" Then she looked over her shoulder to make sure we were still alone and said, "Wow, who knew you were such a dirty girl? I didn't think you had it in you. I'm so proud of you. You go, girl." She started smiling from ear to ear and stared at me with complete admiration. Then she gave me a little pat on the knee and said, "I want to know everything. Is he good in bed?"

"Yes, amazing," I said.

"How big is it, Cindy? C'mon, you have to tell me. I want all the juicy details."

I started to blush. If I don't tell her, then she will keep pressing me for an answer. Realizing who I'm dealing with, I said, "Ugh, okay, but no more questions about it after." I put my hands out and pulled them apart. "This big," I said.

"Wow, Cindy, I am so jealous. Are you sure I can't borrow him for a night?"

"No, you can't borrow him for a night!"

She leaned toward me and, with a soft voice, asked, "Does James know about your steamy affair with the dreamy farmhand?"

My eyes bulged from my head. "What? Of course not, and I would like to keep it that way. As a matter of fact, please don't even mention Anthony to James at all."

"Cindy, you know you don't have to worry about me. If you're sleeping with a hot hunk on the side, I will take it to my grave, sister. I was never here," she assured me, while giving me a wink.

"Earth to Cindy!" Vicky clapped her hands in front of my face and I came back to reality. "Cindy, are you alright, sweetie?"

"Yeah, why?"

She gave me a serious look. "You've been staring out into nothing with a blank face for the last few minutes? I've never seen you zone out like that before. It was kind of creepy. Are you sure you're okay?"

I reassured her, "Yeah, I'm fine. At least, I think I'm fine. Okay, the truth is, I've been having these episodes again where I space out, in a trance. When I get that way, I forget what I'm doing and become disoriented. It's just stress related, I think. What were we talking about?"

"You don't remember?"

"No, I'm so sorry, Vicky."

"It's okay, sweetie. If it continues to happen, please go get checked out. It might be something serious. Now, where were we? Oh yeah, I was telling you what an asshole your husband was for leaving you alone all the time."

"Oh, right, I forgot," I said.

We continued talking for a little while and catching up on things. It felt good to visit with Vicky. I have always looked up to her since college. We get little time to hang out anymore so it was refreshing to have her here. The day seemed to fly by.

Vicky got up and stretched. "I better head out before James gets here. Love ya, girl. Let's do this again, soon." She let out a quick yawn and left.

As I thought about our conversation that day, I became more confused. Did I tell her about Anthony or not? I feel like I did, but she acted as though I didn't. Did she have too much to drink and forget what we talked about? Why can't I make sense of anything? It's so frustrating. I need my brain to hurry and start working again.

I spent the rest of the day drifting in and out of sleep. I tried to watch t.v. a couple of times but my eyes hurt too much and my headache prevented me from so much as trying to listen. All I could do was lie here with my eyes closed and try to fall asleep, while trying to figure out what was really going on.

The nurse visited my room throughout the day. She brought me Jello and some apple juice to get me eating again. It was a struggle for me to swallow the Jello. My throat is still sore from the breathing tube I had. It was almost as difficult to drink my juice. I would take little sips from the straw. As much as my throat hurts and the small appetite I have, the thought of a warm meal is appealing to me. I can't wait to order my first meal from the cafeteria, or should I say, swallow it.

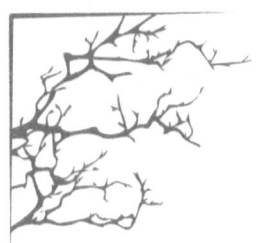

Chapter 3

The following morning, I woke to the sound of a voice I didn't recognize.

"Hi, Cindy, I'm Dr. Lisa. I work with the Mental Health Department. How are you feeling today?"

I yawned and opened my eyes, wiping them with the back of my hand. I took a good look at her. I wanted to tell her to get out, but there was something about her that was comforting. She is soft spoken, and her voice sounds calming. An older woman, close to retiring, I would say. She has short, curly gray hair and glasses that look old-fashioned. A shorter woman with an average build. Her skin has its fair share of wrinkles and a weathered look to it. She looks like someone's grandma. Even her attire was outdated.

I snapped at her. "Mental Health? A shrink? Are you kidding me? Do you people think I'm crazy or something?"

"Cindy, Dr. Smith says you don't remember your accident and your husband also has some concerns about your well-being, so I'm just here to find out what is going on and make sure you're alright?"

I was surprised by what she said to me. Why would she talk to my husband? What does he have to do with any of this?

I glared at her while still trying to wake up and gather my thoughts. "You talked to my husband? Why?"

"Yes, I spoke with him briefly. He came to me with some concerns and I wanted to get his account of what happened the day of your accident," she said.

I can't believe James spoke to a shrink about me. What the hell is wrong with him? It made me angry, but I wanted to hear what he told her about my accident. What he said to me made no sense at all. I would never ride the horses if no one was around, and Anthony would have been home with me. Anthony is always by my side or not too far from me. He would have found me long before James did. I looked right at her, curious to find out what James said to her. "What did he tell you?" I asked.

"He told me he found you in a field with a horse when he got home," she said.

I put my head down. "Yeah, that's the same thing he told me, too." I felt disappointed with what she said. I was hoping to get something different from her than I got from James. Or something slightly different. Maybe some minor detail that confirms James is lying to me.

Dr. Lisa looked at me with sympathetic eyes. The same way a mother would look at her child to comfort them. "Cindy, amnesia is common with the type of injury you suffered from. The brain is a very complex organ and we want to make sure nothing is going on, that is a cause for concern. It's standard procedure to evaluate patients with brain injuries. You have nothing to worry about. You're in excellent hands."

She sat in the chair beside my bed with her legs crossed, holding a notepad and pen, ready to engage me in conversation.

She looked up at me and said, "So tell me, what is the last thing you remember before your accident?"

"The last thing I remember is... I was standing in my kitchen, having another argument with James."

"Did you and your husband argue a lot?"

"Let's just say our marriage has been falling apart for quite some time."

"Okay, Cindy, let's get back to that later. How about we start from the beginning? Tell me about your childhood. Were both of your parents in the home growing up?"

"I had a rough childhood. A lonely childhood. I learned at a young age to take care of myself because my parents were never around."

She asked, "So you were an only child, I assume?"

"Yes, my parents had no interest in having children. I'm pretty sure I was an unplanned pregnancy. They were never home and left me by myself a lot. Both of them had jobs that kept them away, and when they were home, they paid little attention to me. I got sent to my cousin's farm every time I had school vacation or had the summer off from school. I felt like an inconvenience to my parents."

"Did you like going to your cousin's farm?"

"Yes, I loved it. It was an hour's drive outside of the city. It's a beautiful, small ranch with a handful of horses. It's where I learned to ride and it's there I fell in love with a more laid back, simpler way of life. I wanted my own farm one day."

"Cindy, did you and your parents ever go on any family trips or vacations together?"

"No, not once."

"What about school? Did you do well in school? Did you have any friends there?" she asked.

"I got bullied and picked on in school, starting at a young age. There was this one mean girl who picked on me all the time. Whenever she started teasing me, others would join in with her, so I kept to myself while I was in school. I would run home crying and when I would tell my parents what was going on, they would do nothing about it. Gosh, I hated my parents for it. I still hate them both today and I never see it changing."

"So, Cindy, how did you cope with everything you were going through? It must have been hard on you to grow up that way?"

"I'm reluctant to tell you. You're going to think I'm crazy if I do. It's silly, really."

"Cindy, I need you to know that I'm not here to judge you. I'm here to see if you need help and to get you the proper help if need be."

I paused for a moment, thinking it over, and then said, "I had an imaginary friend."

"Tell me about your friend," she said.

"Her name was Brenda. She made me feel good about myself. She made me feel like a person, like I mattered in life and belonged. Brenda was a little older than me and tough. It was like having an older sister. Bullies didn't scare her, and she hated my parents as well. We hung out all the time and talked about everything. She was my best friend... my only friend."

Dr. Lisa turned her eyes toward me. "How long did you continue to have this disorder?"

I almost choked at her question. "What? Disorder? You say it like I'm nuts. She was just an imaginary friend."

"Cindy, I'm not saying you're nuts. I would never say something like that. What you were experiencing is something we call a Dissociative Disorder. Brenda was your escape from reality. Let me ask you something. Is Brenda a real person?"

I put my head down. I knew she was right. I know it's not normal to have an imaginary friend as much as I hate to admit it. "No, Dr. Lisa, Brenda wasn't a real person, but she was always there for me when times were tough, right up until I met my husband. Until then, she was all I had."

Dr. Lisa continued jotting notes down on her notepad. "How did you meet your husband?"

I thought back to when we were both in college. James was a bit of a dork. A handsome one. He was a little taller than me, had light brown hair, a slender build, and a smile that would make me giddy.

He always dressed casually. It fit his personality well. He would wear a nice button up sleeveless shirt, blue jeans and a pair of worn out converse sneakers. He had an easy, carefree look about him that was very comforting to me. His meek personality also attracted me to him. He was soft spoken and very polite.

He was studying to become a tax lawyer on a scholarship, and I was there to appease my parents, who were paying for my college education, unsure of what I wanted to study. The only thing I was certain of was, I wanted to live my life on a farm with the man of my dreams. A simple life. I didn't like the everyday hustle of the city life. It stressed me out to be in a constant rush all the time. And for what? To chase money and miss out on life? I especially didn't want my life to be consumed in that way.

James and I didn't get to know each other well until the second year of college, when I needed a tutor. Studying was not my strong suit, and I needed to do just that in order to graduate. One day when I walked into the library, I saw James sitting by himself at a table near the back. He was busy and focused on whatever work he was doing. I walked over to his table and stood there, not knowing what to say. James started checking me out, looking me up and down, before making eye contact with me. Then he said, "Hi."

I was nervous when I said, "Hi, I'm Cindy."

He gave me a little smile and said, "I'm James. Do you need something, Cindy, or are you just here for my viewing pleasure?"

I blushed, then I stuttered, "I... I was wondering if you knew of anyone that could help me study? I need a tutor."

"Sure, Cindy, I have a couple of free nights during the week if you're interested?"

I got even more nervous and said, "Um, sure."

"Okay, Cindy, give me your number and I will call you. We can start next week."

I gave him my number, feeling shy, and then walked away.

Our relationship started growing at a rapid pace after we began studying together. We were spending more and more time hanging out when we weren't studying and getting closer and closer. I will never forget the first time he kissed me. I was sitting in the grass up against a tree reading a book when he appeared in front of me, startling me. He stood over me and crouched down, almost sitting in my lap. As I looked up at him, that is when he placed his hand on the side of my neck and planted his mouth on mine. His passionate kiss left me dumbfounded. Don't get me wrong, I loved every second. It made our relationship feel official. I didn't feel shy around him anymore. I held his hand when we walked places and kissed him in public. I snuggled up to him when we sat next to each other and made it obvious to everyone that James and I were an item so other girls wouldn't try to pick him up.

It wasn't long before we started becoming intimate with each other. Sex was exciting. We always found fresh places around campus for our encounters, since his roommate spent a lot of time in their dorm, it seemed. Some nights he would take the bus and walk to my house, where I still lived with my parents. He would sneak into my room after they went to bed. We would hang out, fool around, cuddle up together and fall asleep until early morning. He always left before my parents got up for work. It wasn't a big deal, since my parents ignored me and left me to my own vices. I mean, why would they care now? I think they pushed me into college to get me out of the house and ready to start my life somewhere that didn't involve them. I tried to convince James he didn't have to sneak into my room or worry about my mom or dad, but they still made him nervous and he did anything he could to avoid them.

The next few years went great. We were in love and I wanted to spend our lives together forever. James and I got an apartment after graduation. I worked as a secretary for a small office and he got a job at an accounting firm. James was doing great at his job and making a ton of money.

Every day we would get home around the same time or meet up somewhere after work for dinner and spend time out on the town. On the weekends, we would always find things to do together. My favorite was when we would take drives out to the country and sight see the beautiful farms. I enjoyed getting out of the city.

Sometimes we would stop at Ethan's house to visit with him and his new wife, Jody. Ethan and James were close. They've been best friends forever, taking separate paths in life. Ethan went to the Police Academy after high school and was working his way up the chain of command at the local police department, in a small town outside of the city. He was hoping to be chief someday. James was working on his dream of becoming the best lawyer he could be and a partner at his firm. Even though they lived their own busy lives, they still found time to fish together, have a poker night or just a guy's night out on the town.

When James and Ethan get together, I hang out with my bestie, Vicky. I've known Vicky since the start of college. We met at the on-campus coffee shop and clicked right away. She had a lot of spunk. I liked how she was the popular girl in school and I was her best friend. I got a lot of respect from other girls because of my friendship with her. She also made me feel safe. I knew no one would dare pick on me or Vicky would kick their ass.

Vicky was a wild girl who didn't want to get held down with a relationship. At least that's what she always told me. I think she enjoyed sleeping around too much. She took an early financial risk after graduating college and invested in a couple of health clubs. They are successful and bring her a sizable enough income to do what she wants, whether it's traveling, going on vacations or shopping for new jewelry and clothing.

When she worked, and it wasn't often, it was as a personal trainer. She has always been a gym rat and had the body to prove it. She loved her job and got to spend all the time she wanted with hot guys, dating most of them. I honestly believe it was the only reason she would go into work. Whenever I wanted to go out or just have some girl time, it was Vicky I would go see. She was always fun, exciting and the life of the party.

I enjoyed my balanced life with James. I was happy. He seemed happy. Life was good for the time being.

Dr. Lisa continued to write on her notepad and then asked, "What made the two of you decide to get married?"

"It wasn't something we planned together. He sprung it on me and I said yes. I thought I was ready. I mean, I felt ready to commit. Our relationship was going great at that point and I thought he was the one for me."

"Okay, Cindy, give me some insight on what that day was like for you, the day you married James."

One Saturday morning, James woke me up and told me to get ready.

"I'm taking you somewhere," he said.

"Where are you taking me, James?"

"It's a surprise, Cindy."

I murmured, "You know I don't like surprises."

"Well, you just might like this one, so get ready," he said.

I wondered what he might be up to? He seemed thrilled that day and in a rush to get going. I got ready and out the door we went. We got in the car and started heading to wherever we were going. On the way, we stopped by our favorite donut shop for some donuts and coffee. I noticed it was a familiar route we took when we went to the country.

"James, are we taking another drive through the country today?"

"I'm not telling you anything. It's a surprise I told you," he said.

We drove down a lot of dirt roads for a while after driving through a small town. I was admiring the rolling hills of grass and the beautiful wildflowers until we came to a long dirt driveway. James slowed down and turned into the driveway that seemed to go on forever. As we neared the end, we came upon a beautiful ranch-style house. There were white fences and gates everywhere. A greenhouse sat off to one side of the house and a big two-story barn sat on the other side toward the back. There were fields of grass everywhere.

"This place is beautiful, James. Who lives here?"

James grabbed me by the hand and started walking me to the big open farmer's porch. I couldn't help but look through one of the big picture windows that lined the front of the house. The place wasn't empty. Furniture filled the entire home.

I got aggressive with my tone. "James! What is going on? Where are we? What are we doing here and who lives here?" That's when he placed both of my hands into his and got down on his knee. I thought to myself, "Oh my gosh, is this happening right now?" James looked up at me, held my hands and started talking.

"Cindy, I love you with all of my being, and I can't imagine spending any of my life without you. Will you marry me and be my wife?"

My eyes welled up, and I did my best to hold back the tears, but I failed to do so. "Yes! I will marry you!"

James reached into his front pocket and pulled out a ring. He then placed it on my finger. He stood up, and we hugged for what seemed like forever.

I pressed him again. "So, why are we here? And again, who lives here?"

"Cindy, I didn't want to tell you until I got you to say yes to marrying me and getting a yes from you wasn't very hard, by the way," he joked.

"I'm still waiting for an answer, James."

Then he reached into his other pocket and pulled out a key ring with a plastic tag and two keys on it. He held them up and handed them to me.

"Welcome home," he said.

"Wait! What? Are you frigging kidding me? This isn't funny, James! This... this is ours? Did you buy this house?"

"Yes, I bought it. It's ours."

I stood there in a stupor, astonished by everything that had just happened. I rushed over to the door and put the key in. I unlocked the door and stepped inside.

It was a beautiful home. Modern, yet rustic enough to fit in with a farm life. It was a lot bigger inside than it looked from the outside. It was an open concept with the living room, dining room and kitchen sharing a space that was only separated by kitchen counters. Down the hall past the kitchen, there was a door to the basement, guest bedroom, bathroom, and laundry room. At the other end of the house, there was a main bedroom with a bathroom and a smaller bedroom next to it that James turned into his office.

In the dining room area, there was a back door that went to a big screened-in porch that had a patio table and chairs. Outside in the backyard was a stone patio with a fire pit as its centerpiece with lounge chairs. The view was amazing. There is an enormous field with shelters for horses that get turned out to pasture, long white wooden fences running around the property, and a big red barn that brought the entire landscape together.

"Come on James. Let's go see the barn."

I slid the giant doors open and smiled as I looked around. There were six horse stalls lined on each side, a spacious tack room with a utility sink and a stairway that led up to a top floor hay loft. The smell of the barn was familiar to me from my time spent at my cousin's farm growing up. The smell of hay, pine shavings and horses still filled the place. It smelled so amazing and brought back many fond memories.

We walked upstairs to the hayloft. It was empty except for some old bales of hay that made up a small pile near the door used to bring hay up into the loft. I opened the door and took in the view. "This is so beautiful, James. What an amazing day!"

We spent the next few weekends moving stuff from the apartment to our new home. It didn't take much effort since we didn't have to furnish the house. James said he had a designer furnish it so it would be move-in ready for us. We pretty much only had to pack up our clothes, personal belongings and some miscellaneous items we couldn't live without. Most of the stuff we didn't take with us we donated or threw away.

We wed at our new home. A small country style wedding in our yard, with our close friends. Ethan was James's best man, and Vicky was my bridesmaid. White table cloths and flowers adorned the backyard. Our wedding resembled a small family, weekend get together, just how we wanted it, simple.

We were married under an arched trellis covered in white flowers. I wore a beautiful short white country style dress, a tiara and a pair of new cowgirl boots. James wore a fancy dress shirt, a pair of denim jeans, and black dress shoes. It was a perfect day.

We settled into our new home. James was making enough money at his job, so he insisted I leave my job to stay home and focus on the farm, which I did.

After moving into our new home, I got a few horses and some chickens. I spent my days doing farm chores, keeping the house in order and growing vegetables in our garden. I was enjoying my new life on the farm. For a while, I was happy. Being a stay at home wife was something new to me, but I enjoyed it. I took good care of James since he had to work all the time and I kept the house in order. Dinner was always ready for him when he got home every night. I would cook him breakfast and lunch too on his days off. I enjoyed taking care of him. Then things started taking a turn for the worse. It wasn't long after moving into the house when our marriage started deteriorating.

"That will be enough for today, Cindy. I meet with patients once a week, but Dr. Smith would like some feedback as soon as possible. I'm thinking we can do this daily to get things moving, as long as you are feeling well enough. Get some rest and I will see you tomorrow around the same time," she said. Then she gathered her notes and papers, and exited my room.

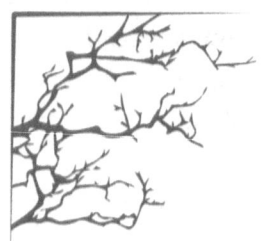

Chapter 4

Even though I just spent time talking about James and a time in our relationship that was good, I had no interest in thinking about it or him. My mind started thinking about my one true love, my soulmate Anthony. My heart and my body ached for him. I thought about the first time we had sex and how amazing it was. I remember it like it was yesterday, and it makes me miss him so much.

As I thought about Anthony, I started daydreaming about our first time. I will never forget it... I climbed into bed one night and got turned down by James again. This has been going on for a long time now and I couldn't take it anymore. It only reinforced my craving for Anthony. It made me angry to get rejected by my husband all the time. I have had enough. I will show him, I thought.

The next morning, after James left for work, I slid out of bed and picked out clothes that were worthy of seduction and would get Anthony's attention. Cowgirl boots, low cutoff jean shorts and a tight white tank top so thin you could see through it. I slipped on a pair of soft white cotton panties, my shorts, boots and top with no bra, so my breasts were visible through the fabric. I brushed my teeth, put my hair in a ponytail, and went in search of him.

As I walked through the living room, he caught my eye out the window. He was fixing a fence gate in the backyard. Standing there in tight, light blue, worn out denim jeans with no shirt and the sun beating down on his muscular, toned body and his sun kissed, tanned complexion. His hair was a little messy from running his fingers through it to keep it in place. I couldn't help but notice the bulge in his pants. Yummy, it sent excitement rushing through my body.

Okay, am I doing this? I asked myself. What if Anthony rejects me? He obviously knows I'm married, my husband hired him. Or worse, what if he tells James? Am I over thinking things? I see the way he checks me out when he thinks I'm not looking and I'm pretty sure when I overheard him talking on the phone once, saying "she's a hot little blonde," he was referring to me? I mean, I'm short and fit, with dirty blonde hair. Even if he wasn't referring to me, he thought some blonde girl was hot, and it's pretty obvious I'm blonde. Also, he has been flirting with me for months now, undressing me with his eyes and being especially nice to me. I can tell he wants me just as much as I want him. Yup, I'm doing this. If I do nothing, then it's just going to drive me crazy to be around him, and I will regret not trying. I need to make the first move.

I went to the back door and called for him. I was almost trembling with fear and excitement as I watched him walking toward the house. "Don't chicken out now, Cindy," I said. I overcame my fear by thinking about how I'm getting back at James for his constant neglect of me and how mad I was at him for making me feel so unwanted. I told myself I needed this. I deserved this. If my husband won't give me the attention I crave, then I will get it on my own, somewhere else.

When Anthony stepped through the door, I watched his eyes look me up and down. He seemed in awe of how I looked, standing in front of him.

"Cindy, do you need something?" he asked.

I pushed the door closed and stepped closer to him, placing my hand on his chest. I leaned into him, pressing my breasts up against him, and whispered into his ear, "Yes, I need a favor from you."

He looked shocked by how I was presenting myself to him. It almost seemed like a struggle for him to reply to me. Then he said, "Anything for you."

I looked right into his eyes. My bright blue eyes pierced him. "Good," I said. I ran my hand down his hard abs, admiring his body and soft skin. I slid my fingers down behind his waistband. Wow! He's not wearing any underwear. That's so hot, I thought. I felt his smooth, shaved skin on my fingers as I pushed my hand into his pants. I started kissing his chest and working my way up to his neck. The smell of his cologne was intoxicating. I tugged at his pants, pulling him closer to me, as I planted my lips on his mouth. I kissed him and he kissed me back. He tasted amazing, and he was enjoying my advances toward him. I was so turned on at this point I couldn't take it anymore. I gazed at him with my bedroom eyes. "Anthony, can I get that favor from you now?"

"Of course. What do you need?"

I turned my head and looked down the hall to direct his attention there. I almost spoke in a whimper as I begged him with my voice. "Please take me to the bedroom."

He turned me toward the door, placed his hands on my hips from behind, and walked me down the hall toward the bedroom.

About an hour later, I stood there in the bedroom doorway. Naked, holding my clothes, still panting and trying to catch my breath, while covered in his sweat. My hair was a complete mess, and I smelled like him. My legs shook, and I felt a little dizzy, which is why I stood there, trying to regain my composure. He wore me out to the point of exhaustion.

I still couldn't believe what had just happened. I never felt so satisfied in my life or so pleasured. Anthony and I were so in tune with each other and so compatible in bed, I swear we were meant for one another. I have never been loud during sex before. I never had a reason to be. The loud moans of involuntary, pleasurable screams he could seduce out of me were pure bliss. It felt so unreal, like a dream. I never had that kind of connection with my husband, James. I was in awe of Anthony and if there was one thing I was certain of... I was going to continue to crave him and want more.

I was in my room, getting dressed and thinking about what had just happened. I felt a little guilty for a moment. Am I going to keep doing this to James? How would I feel if he did this to me? Then I snapped out of it. As a matter of fact, I don't think I care at this point. He doesn't appreciate me anymore. I mean, I love him, but I'm not in love with him now. Why should I care about him when he doesn't care about me? If I'm being honest with myself, the rush I got from cheating on him was exciting and I felt like I was getting some well-deserved revenge on the person who was hurting me. I wasn't about to walk away from Anthony, the one person who brought me happiness and gave me a reason to want to keep living.

"Cindy...Cindy...hey, there you are. Are you okay?" the nurse said to me, looking troubled.

"Yeah, why?" I asked.

"I've been trying to get your attention for the last few minutes and you were just laying there, staring out into nothing and not responding to me. I will have to let the doctors know."

"Oh, I'm so sorry. I was daydreaming about something and I guess I was deep in thought."

"Cindy, I understand, but I'm going to run it by them anyway, just to be safe and make sure it has nothing to do with your injury. We want you to get better, not worse."

"Okay," I said.

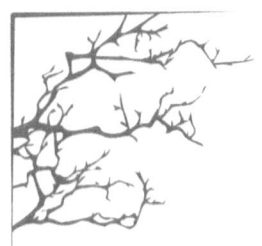

Chapter 5

The following day, Dr. Lisa came to see me again. I was already awake and trying to eat my breakfast of Jello, scrambled eggs and grape juice. She sat down in her usual spot with her notepad.

"Good morning, Cindy. How are you feeling today? Are you ready to pick up where we left off yesterday?"

I was lying to her when I said, "I guess so." I really didn't want to talk to her at all.

"Cindy, before we get to where we left off, I want to ask you about what happened yesterday? The nurse informed me you were in some sort of trance when she came in, and it took her a few minutes to get you to respond to her. Does this happen often and how long has it been going on for?"

"It only happens once in a while. It's been going on for as long as I can remember and I don't know why it happens. I just start thinking about something and I space out in sort of a trance. I'm not sure how long it lasts. It could be minutes or it could be hours. I'm not sure."

"Are you aware of your surroundings when you get like that?" she asked.

"No, I don't hear or see anything other than what is going on in my mind. When I get like that, I block everything out. Sometimes, a loud noise snaps me back to reality."

"Interesting. Okay, Cindy, let's pick up where we left off yesterday. You said your marriage went downhill. Tell me about that."

"After we moved into the house and James convinced me to quit my job, I realized how lonely I was, being home by myself all the time. James was always working, and I started feeling depressed from the isolation. I felt trapped. It felt like I was living with my parents again."

"It wasn't much better when he was home. He neglected me all the time, physically and emotionally. He never initiated sex with me, and when I would make any advances toward him, he would turn me down. We no longer went out on dates like we used to. He stopped showing me affection and spending time with me. James was one hundred percent checked out of our marriage. He spent most of his time at home on the weekends working in his office. His job became his priority, and it consumed all of his time. I couldn't get him to help me do anything around the farm. I started losing my mind. We began arguing quite a lot. I went from being his everything to being his nothing and feeling invisible to him. I was ready to give up, end my marriage, and move on. That's when James hired Anthony to help me around the farm, and it changed my life."

"Cindy, when I spoke with your husband, he said you mentioned someone by that name. He also said he didn't know of anyone named Anthony, and you seemed very confused to him. Tell me your side of the story. Who is Anthony?"

"Frankly, James is lying. He is a liar, and he is the one who hired Anthony. Anthony is so amazing. I love him and as soon as I get out of here, I am divorcing James and marrying Anthony."

"Have you spoken to your husband about your intentions?"

"No, I have not. Something inside of me is telling me not to trust James. I'm still very confused about a lot of things and I just get a bad feeling when I'm around him."

Dr. Lisa paused for a moment. "So tell me about Anthony and how he became involved in your life."

I thought back. I remember it very well. James and I were having another argument.

I started yelling at him, "I can't take it anymore, James! You're never home and I'm home alone all the time while you're at work. You only come here to sleep or work in your office. You're always too tired to do anything with me or too tired to go out on dates like we always did before. We don't have sex. You spend your days off working on your laptop because your job is all you care about now! I'm sick and tired of being alone all the time with no one to talk to, and you know what else, James? I'm sick of this place as well. If I wanted to be ignored or be lonely all the time, I would have stayed living with my parents instead of starting a life with you."

He screamed at me, "What the fuck do you want me to do? My job pays the bills and keeps us living in this house!"

"James, in case you haven't noticed, I don't care anymore. What was once my dream has now become my hell. I don't want to be here anymore, and I don't want to be with you." That's when I broke down and sobbed. I couldn't hold back the tears that started pouring down my cheeks. I felt trapped and alone.

He stood there frustrated and angry that I would even dare start another fight over this again, but once he saw me crying, his demeanor changed. He walked over and hugged me. "Cindy, I didn't realize things had gotten this bad between us."

I pulled it together and wiped away my tears. "It's too much for me, James. Not only am I home alone all the time, the farm is getting to be too much. There are too many things that need done, I just can't do. Fences need fixed, hay needs stacked, heavy wheelbarrows of manure need moved, repairs need done, etc. These are jobs for a man and it's too overwhelming for me. We wanted this life together and now your job consumes all of your time while I stay at home... alone. We are pretty much roommates now, living separate lives."

James stood there gazing at me, looking sorrowful. He placed his hands on my arms and said, "What if I hired someone to help you around here during the week when I'm not home? Paul at work has his brother staying with him for a while. He lives up north and comes down here for the winter months to find work. He's a carpenter or a handyman, something like that. I could talk to Paul and see if his brother would be interested."

"James, you would do that for me?"

"Yes, of course. I will talk to him tomorrow."

The morning Anthony started working for me, he pulled up in a pickup truck. It was a newer truck but looked worn out. You could tell he used it for work with the amount of dings and scratches that were all over it. It had big cargo tool boxes in the back and a roof rack with ladders stacked up on it.

I opened the front door and went out onto the porch to greet him. I watched as he stepped out of his truck and placed his worn out brown leather cowboy boots on the ground while I stood there in awe, looking him over.

He was wearing snug denim jeans and a flannel shirt that was unbuttoned at the top, with his sleeves rolled up. He was lean, with a toned body. His face was handsome and clean shaved. He was dreamy, manly, and around my age. He looked like the perfect guy you would read about in a romance novel or someone who could jump off of a wild horse to scare off a dangerous animal. A real man. A man's man. Not someone who wears a suit and shines a seat with his ass all day like my husband does. Anthony looked like the kind of man you want by your side when there's trouble or when you feel frightened. Someone you call for help, knowing he will rush to your aid and take care of the problem. He looked tough. He looked sexy. He looked... perfect.

I could see him sizing me up and checking out my figure. I don't think he noticed my new shiny boots or wavy blonde hair at all. When his dark eyes met my bright eyes, it was like time stood still. It felt like we were gazing into each other's souls.

He walked over to shake my hand. "Hi, I'm Anthony," he said.

He had a nice firm grip and I could tell that he worked with his hands just by how rough his skin felt. "I'm Cindy," I replied.

We both continued to look one another over, admiring what we both saw. The smell of the cologne that radiated from his body turned me on. He smelled delicious. I wanted to devour him. "Anthony, let me show you around so you get an idea of what needs to be done," I said.

I couldn't contain my smile and it made me feel like such a teenager. As a matter of fact, I don't think I stopped smiling at him the whole day. I just kept gazing into his eyes and smiling.

I'm pretty sure he knew I was into him, the same way I could tell he was into me. Never before has anyone undressed me with their eyes in such depth as he did that day. He wanted to know what was hiding under my clothing just as much as I wanted to know what was hiding under his. We both made it pretty obvious.

We spent the better half of the day talking while I showed him around the farm. It was refreshing to have someone to converse with and someone handsome to gawk at all day. He was charming, polite and very attractive. Thinking back to the day Anthony showed up here, I know for a fact I would have slept with him that very day if I had the chance. I mean, if you saw him, you would too. Yup, he's that electrifying to look at. Beautiful. Delicious even.

It was nice to sleep in most days since James hired Anthony to help around the farm. He was a carpenter when there was work available and we had plenty of work to be done on our horse farm. If we ever run out of things to do, I'm pretty sure I can make up some stuff to keep him around. There is no way I'm letting him leave me as long as I can help it.

My life has been easier and not so overwhelming since Anthony got here. There is more time on my hands and I spend it watching him, mostly. I can't keep my eyes off of him and I want him so bad it's painful. I look for any reason or excuse to interact with him throughout the day as he is working. It almost feels like I'm being a pest, although I can't help it. I'm attracted to him like a magnet. He doesn't seem to mind either. I even rush to get my house chores done just so I can be outside with him.

After a few months of getting to know Anthony and flirting with each other nonstop, I got up enough courage and threw myself at him. It was the best decision I ever made. It was mind blowing, and it was the start of a relationship that continued to grow to a great extent. I thought I would feel horrible for doing such a thing behind James's back, but I didn't. As a matter of fact, I felt the exact opposite. It felt invigorating, and I wanted to keep doing it. What I didn't know at the time was how head over heels in love with Anthony I was going to get. I became obsessed with him.

A couple days after my first sexual encounter with Anthony, I was lying on the couch daydreaming when the sound of boots walking across the back porch interrupted my thoughts. I felt a rush of excitement come over me. I watched as the doorknob turned and the door opened. Anthony poked his head in, looking for me.

"Cindy?"

"Yes? I'm right here, come in." I sat up, ready to engage him.

He looked over at me and said in a quiet voice, "Is James home yet?"

"No, he shouldn't be home for a couple of hours. Why, what's up?"

He walked over, sat down next to me, and placed his hand on my leg. "I can't stop thinking about the other day, and I can't stop thinking about you," he said.

I smiled. "I can't stop thinking about you either, Anthony."

Then he got up, grabbed me by the hand, pulled me up off of the couch and walked me down to the bedroom, where it all started.

A short while later, I felt like I was floating on a cloud. I never felt so alive in my life. So satisfied. So full of joy. I put my clothes back on and stepped out of the room, closing the door behind me while Anthony got dressed. My feelings of joy came to a crashing halt when I walked down the hallway and saw James sitting on the couch, practically slumped over.

"James? When did you get home?" I said loud enough so Anthony could hear me from the bedroom.

He sat there looking troubled, with a long look on his face. "We need to talk, Cindy. But first I need a drink." He stood up and made his way to his office.

Looking down the hall, I saw Anthony peering out the door. I waved him out with my hand, and he scurried down the hall and out the back door. I heard his truck start and watched him through the front window drive away. I made my way over to the couch and sat down. I felt like I was going to faint. How long was James sitting on the couch for? Did he hear us in the bedroom? I was so loud. I'm sure the sound of my shrieking moans and Anthony's hips smacking up against my body echoed throughout the house. How could he not hear us? I was panicking and I could feel my heart pounding in my chest. I thought I was going to get sick. I really screwed up, I thought.

I sat there, nervous and waiting for James to walk back out to the living room. It was so quiet I could hear him pouring a second drink. "This can't be good," I said to myself. He walked back into the living room, still holding his drink in his hand. He took a long look at me while he sat in the chair across from me. After he took a big swig of whiskey, he put his head down, staring into his lap.

I stuttered, "What's going on, James?"

He lifted his head and looked at me with a blank stare, as if he was looking right through me. "Cindy, I don't know how to say this to you."

"Come on, James, spit it out. You're making me nervous. Please, James." I was waiting for him to drop what felt like a bomb on me, telling me it was over and that he wanted me gone.

Then he spoke. "I got a huge promotion at work today."

I almost screeched. "What? A promotion? That's what you wanted to talk to me about?" I was still trying to calm myself down. He looked disappointed having to tell me the news. I felt relieved it wasn't about what Anthony and I were just doing in the bedroom.

"Yes," he said.

"That is great, James. Congratulations. That's very exciting news."

James started getting nervous and began to fidget with his glass. His face got flush, and it looked like he was going to start sweating. "The problem is, Cindy, it requires me to travel a great deal. I will be home even less than I am now. We already fight enough over it. I don't know what to do?"

As I thought about it and processed what he just told me, I felt good about him leaving. I didn't care anymore. Anthony will be here during the days to keep me company and satisfied, I thought, as I was smiling inside. Then it hit me and the shock set in. I snapped at him, "No way, James! You're never home as it is and now you want me to stay in this house at night, all by myself, in the middle of nowhere? Are you out of your mind?"

He snapped back at me, "I have my guns in the closet. I taught you how to use them."

I got angry. "What? Is that what you want? Your wife, terrified and alone at night, sleeping with a gun? Seriously! I can't take much more of this. I'm questioning whether we should stay married at this point."

"Cindy, what about Anthony?"

"What about him, James? Do you think he can get here in time if something goes wrong in the middle of the night? Do you think it will keep me from being scared all night? Whatever, I will just go to Vicky's place each night you're gone and stay with her. Anthony can drop me off and pick me up each day."

James looked nervous. "No, Cindy, you can't burden Vicky with our problems. Not only that, I don't think she is home much, either. You will just be alone at her place, too. I was thinking about asking Anthony if he will just stay here full time. We have the guest bedroom and there's plenty of room here. He can stay with us instead of staying at his brother's place. It will also save him a couple hours of travel time each day and there will always be someone here with you. You won't have to be alone while I'm away. Why don't you talk to him about it tomorrow? I'm sure he won't mind. As long as you're okay with him being here?"

I couldn't believe what I just heard. Did he just suggest my lover stay here with us right down the hall, in the same house as me? It was a struggle to hold my excitement inside. I said in a calm voice, "Okay, I will talk to him about it and see what he thinks."

I could hardly sleep that night thinking about Anthony staying here full time. Now I couldn't wait for James to leave. I was looking forward to his traveling and being gone. Anthony and I can have the house to ourselves when James isn't here. We can run around with no clothes on if we want, shower together, make love, hang out, snuggle, and best of all, sleep in the same bed together. I look forward to that the most. It's been so long since I have been able to fall asleep in someone's arms. I long to be held and feel the comfort of a man. I need to feel secure and safe. I couldn't wait.

I fell asleep after lying awake for most of the night thinking about Anthony. It seemed to be only minutes of sleep before I woke up to the sound of a truck pulling up to the house. I jumped out of bed and looked out the window. It was Anthony. I slipped into a tee shirt and a pair of gym shorts, then rushed to the door to catch him before he went out back.

I stepped out onto the porch and ran over to greet him with a smile and a hug that I needed desperately. "Hey good-looking, I got something to ask you."

"I know," he said.

"You know?"

"Yes, James called me early this morning and discussed it with me already."

"Oh, he did? Well, what did you tell him?"

"I told him he couldn't pay me enough to stay with you." Then he smiled, smacked me on the ass and opened the door to his truck.

"Ha ha. That's hilarious, Anthony."

He reached into his truck, pulled out a suitcase, looked at me and said, "So, are you going to help me unpack?"

I gave him a smile and said, "You couldn't pay me enough." Then I stuck out my ass, shook it at him playfully, and went back into the house.

"That is how Anthony became involved in my life and how he began staying with us."

"Okay," Dr. Lisa said. "Let's stop here for today and pick back up where we left off tomorrow. I will see you again in the morning."

Later in the day, James came to visit me.

"Hi, honey, how are you feeling today?" he asked.

"Don't you 'honey' me, James!"

"Cindy, what's wrong with you? Are you okay?"

"I will tell you what's wrong with me. You went running your mouth behind my back to the doctor, telling him I'm crazy! Now I have to tell my life story to a psychiatrist every day to prove I'm not. What is wrong with you, James? Who do you think you are, to take it upon yourself, to think you know what is best for me? Are you trying to get me admitted so they keep me locked up in this frigging hospital? I'm sure that's exactly what you're trying to do. Then you can just live your life, as you have been doing since our marriage, without the headache of having me around."

"Cindy, I am just concerned for you and I want what's best for you. I'm worried and want to make sure you're alright. You were asking me about an imaginary friend of yours. I thought you would have gotten over that kind of stuff years ago. I want you to get help before it's too late, and this is the perfect place for you to get help while you're here."

"James, do you want to know what's best for me? Do you want to know what will help me? I need you to do something for me."

"What, Cindy? Whatever you need."

I looked at James like I wanted to kill him and said, "Turn around and walk back out the door. I can't even stand to look at you right now. I don't want to hear another word out of your mouth. Just leave James. You think I'm crazy? I will give you crazy. Get the fuck out!"

He turned around to leave and paused for a few seconds to look back at me. His glare was full of rage, like he wanted to strangle me. I thought he was going to reach out his hand and choke me. His face turned bright red as he clenched his fists tight. His reaction made me feel very uneasy. Then he turned around and walked out the door, never looking back.

The rest of my day was pretty boring. I was getting restless laying in bed. I hope soon I can get up and go for a walk or go outside for a little while and enjoy the fresh air. I started to fall asleep again. I felt someone grab me by the shirt and pull, startling me. "Cindy! Get up! You need to wake up!"

I opened my eyes. "Anthony, is that really you?"

"Yes, it's me, my love."

Words started spilling from my mouth as I got frantic. "Oh my gosh, Anthony. If you only knew how much I have missed you. I knew you would come for me. I can't stop thinking about you or us because I love you so much. They think I'm crazy. James and Vicky said they don't know who you are. They are lying. Did you come to get me out of here? You can't leave here without me. I don't care what James will think. I am going to divorce him right away so we can be together forever."

He leaned into me and started kissing me like he wanted to consume me. I missed the taste of his lips on mine. His smell and touch were a welcome comfort to me. I wrapped my arms around him and held onto him like I would never let him go. I calmed down, then Anthony looked at me with a disturbing, troubled look on his face and I didn't like it. It was alarming and frightening to see.

He sat down on my bed and placed his hand on the side of my face, the other on my lap. "Cindy, you know I love you more than life itself and I can't go on without you, but you need to listen to me carefully. James found out about us and he's threatening to kill me. He is extremely dangerous. I keep getting away from him, but he keeps finding me somehow. There's no going back home and risking my roommate getting hurt. I'm unsure of what to do. He plans on killing you, too. You need to stay away from him. We both need to get away when you get out. I can't stay. I have to leave, but I will come back for you, my love. Right now you need to stay here, where you are safe from him, until I can figure something out." Then he let go and pulled away from me. He gave me one last look and headed for the door.

I cried out, "Anthony, where are you going? No, please don't leave me again. Anthony! Please come back, I need you. Baby, don't go." Why would he leave me here and not take me with him? I died inside, watching him walk out the door.

"Ah!" I screamed as I woke up weeping and very shaken. I wiped the tears that were streaming down my face. Oh my gosh, it was just a nightmare. It felt so real, just like the other one. All I could do was lie here trembling and trying to process what had just happened. I didn't sleep well the rest of the night.

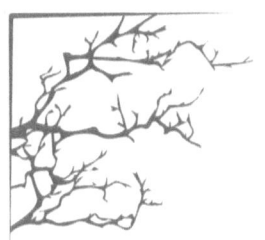

Chapter 6

I wasn't looking forward to meeting with Dr. Lisa today. I still wasn't over my nightmare about Anthony. It still haunted me. I felt drained, especially after not getting a good night's rest. I hoped she wouldn't show up, but, like clockwork, she did, and it annoyed me.

Dr. Lisa got right into it with me as soon as she walked in. She sat down and said, "Today, I want you to start off by telling me more about your time with Anthony. What was it like? How did the two of you spend your days together?"

I thought back, and I remembered when there were a few weeks before James had his first trip. It went by slowly. Anthony and I hung out while he worked, flirting, using playful banter on one another, and talking about everything. I felt so comfortable expressing myself to him and I could talk about anything with Anthony. I could tell him things about myself I wouldn't even dare to share with my husband.

When I wasn't busy bothering him, I would lie out in one of the lounge chairs by the fire pit and turn myself on, watching him work. I couldn't help it. I am so attracted to him.

Anthony and I had sex every chance we could. We were like hormonal crazed teenagers exploring each other's body and ravaging each other until complete and total satisfaction.

I was counting down the days until James leaves. Only two more days and then I get two weeks alone with Anthony. Just him and I, alone together. It's going to be so amazing falling asleep with him and waking up next to him. I want to feel the warmth of his body next to mine.

Time seemed to stand still until the morning James left for his first work trip. He got ready, grabbed his suitcase I packed for him and gave me an unsuspecting kiss on the way out the door, which I wiped off with disgust, after he turned around to walk away.

I yelled to him, "Have a great trip and call me when you land, so I know you made it there safe and sound."

He yelled back, "Okay," then got into his car and drove off.

I knew he would make it there. I just wanted to know when he was far away and gone, so I didn't have to worry about being caught with Anthony alone. I patiently waited all day for him to call, wondering if he would or not. When he didn't, I started beating myself up over it. Did he forget? Is he not there yet? Does he not plan on calling me? What the hell is his problem?

It was a little after eight o'clock that night when I got the call I have been desperately needing. His plane just landed, and he was on his way to his hotel room.

I walked around the house in a hurry, shutting off any lights that were left on, and making sure I locked the doors and windows. Then I went into Anthony's room, shut the door behind me and locked it. Anthony was already in bed and falling asleep. I took off my clothes and slipped under the sheets with him.

"Um, you still have your underwear on, Mr. Buzz Kill. Those don't belong in bed with me. Take them off," I ordered him.

He reached under the covers and removed them. I snuggled right up to him, resting my face on his chest. My arm was over his body, holding him, and I had one leg up over his. It felt so amazing to have someone to hold, to snuggle up to and be affectionate with. Also, having someone to hold me, who wanted me, who enjoyed spending time with me. A real man, who not only accepts my sexual advances, he pursues me. He invests his time in me and carries on conversations with me. He makes me feel needed and important to him. I craved his attention. I needed his affirmation and affection, his approval, his time and his touch. And the sex, oh my gosh, did I mention the sex? He has an insatiable appetite for it, just as I do, and it is amazing and satisfying.

I slept so well up against Anthony's warm, soft skin, listening to his beating heart through his chest while I laid my head on him. I could feel every breath he took while he slept. There was no getting close enough to him. All I wanted was to be wrapped up in him.

I haven't slept that good in as long as I can remember. Waking up next to him with his arm over me had me in pure bliss. I had a serious addiction, and he was my drug. As soon as I moved, I heard his soft voice. "Good morning, gorgeous. I've been waiting for you to wake up."

I turned my head to look at him and said, "Oh, have you?"

He responded, "I hate to do this because I want to stay right here with you, but I have to get out there and feed the animals. You were sleeping so peacefully I didn't want to move and wake you." Then he started kissing his way down my face until he reached my lips to get a taste of me.

"No," I pouted. "Don't leave me."

"Sorry, but I have to," he said.

He tried to get up, and I pushed him back down. I climbed over his legs and pinned him there. I started kissing him all over, getting him fully aroused. I looked up at him and said, "I hate to do this to you, but if you want more of that later, then you need to go to town with me today. I need your truck." Then I gave him a big, playful smile and jumped off of the bed.

"What!" he said. "You're just going to leave me here like this and walk away?"

I smiled at him and said, "Hmm, let me think. What was it someone just said to me? Oh yeah, that's right...Sorry, but I have to. Have fun trying to get it in your pants." I continued to smile at him while he laid there looking at me. I stopped, stuck my ass out at him and gave it a good slap to tease him even more, then I walked away giggling.

I enjoy teasing and enticing Anthony. I love the look on his handsome face and the way he looks at me when he wants me bad enough. It brings out his assertive male behavior. The longer I make him wait and the more I tease him, the more he would dominate and control me when I let him have me. He was my predator, and I was his prey. He was going to hunt me down until he pounced on me, and that is what he did.

I was heading to the front door and almost there when I heard him come up behind me. He reached around me, placed his hand on my throat, and gently started squeezing. It sent shivers through my body.

"Where do you think you're going?" he asked.

He pushed me up against the door and had his way with me. It was amazing. Once he was done with me, he whispered in my ear, "Now we can feed the animals and go to town."

After what he just did, who was I to protest anything he says? Heck, he can say or do whatever he likes to me. As soon as I caught my breath, I said, "Okay, Anthony."

I enjoyed the drive to town. I drove while he had his hand placed on my leg, holding my thigh the whole drive. It made my heart flutter. That is something James never did to me, not once, all the times we were in a vehicle together.

We talked a little on the ride to town about raised garden beds. He knew I needed one and wanted to get the project started for me. As we continued to drive, Anthony got quiet. I could tell he was still tired.

"Why don't you put the seat back and take a little nap?" I said.

He responded, "Okay, baby, I think I will. I sure could use a nap." He laid down on the seat and dozed off.

I thought to myself, Oh... my... gosh. Did he just call me "baby?" Yes, he did. I wanted to bounce up and down in my seat, but I withheld my excitement. "Baby," I said to myself. It has a nice ring to it. No, it has a beautiful ring to it. I don't think I stopped smiling all the way to the store. I felt like I was on top of the world.

I pulled into the feed and grain store, backed up to the loading dock, and shut the truck off. I rubbed his leg with my hand. "Hey, you handsome man, are you going into the store with me or do you want to keep resting?"

"Of course I'm going in with you," he said.

As we walked together into the store, I thought about holding his hand. I wanted to, but I fought the urge. We didn't need anyone seeing us hold hands. I could only imagine the rumors that would spread around town like wildfire. It would only be a matter of time before something like that made its way back to James. We walked around, seeing if there was anything other than horse and chicken feed we needed to get.

"Hey, Anthony, check this thing out. It's one of those buzzer things you put at the entrance of a driveway and it warns you when someone drives up. Do you think we should get it?"

"Hey, Cindy."

"Oh, hey Bill."

Bill was an older gentleman who worked at the store. He's been here forever and knows everybody in town. If you wanted some local gossip, Bill would be happy to indulge you.

"I saw you talking to yourself and thought you might need help with something?"

"No, Bill, I'm fine. I was just showing Anthony this thing here and asking him if we should get it for the house."

Bill asked, "Who's Anthony?"

"Bill, this is Anthony."

I turned around to introduce him to Bill, and he was no longer standing there. "Sorry Bill, he was here just a second ago. Anthony works for me. James hired him to do some maintenance and projects around the farm."

"Oh, I'm sorry, Cindy. I was confused. I didn't see you walk in with anyone, but it has been a long morning and I wasn't paying any attention to who was walking in. Maybe you can introduce us another time? Anyway, how is James doing? I never see him anymore. Heck, it's been quite some time since I've seen him last."

"He's fine. He works a lot and recently got a promotion, which requires him to travel most of the time."

"Well, tell him Bill from the Grain Store said hello and congratulations when you see him. I'm going to make sure someone is loading up the feed you ordered."

"Anthony! Anthony!" I kept calling out as I walked around the store, looking for him. Then I thought maybe he went back out to the truck and was waiting for me there. I went up to the counter, paid for my stuff, and walked out to the truck.

That's strange, he's not here. I moved the truck over into a closer parking space, away from the loading dock, so he could see me when he came out. I wondered, maybe he is in the bathroom? Or maybe he bumped into his brother and went to help him with something?

Almost an hour passed by and now I'm panicking. I called his phone multiple times, and it just rang with no answer. I drove around town for hours, stopping to look through shop windows for him, checking all the side streets and asking random people if they had seen him. I gave up and headed home. The drive took forever. I couldn't stop crying and wondering if he was okay. He will show up at some point, I hope.

I pulled up to the house and went inside to look for him. He wasn't there. I checked the backyard, calling out for him, and he was nowhere to be found. I went back inside and curled up on the couch, waiting for him to call me back or walk through the front door. I ended up crying myself to sleep.

I woke up, and it was late. I panicked again over Anthony. Looking down the hall, I noticed his bedroom door was closed. Right away I rushed down to his room and opened his door to peek in and there he was, in bed and sound asleep. I was so relieved at the sight of him. I wanted to curl up next to him, but he looked so peaceful and comfortable I didn't dare disturb him. I shut his door and went to my bed, once again smiling and happy.

Dr. Lisa cut me off. "Where was Anthony, Cindy? It seems kind of strange that he would just disappear on you. Did you ask yourself why someone would go with you and then vanish without a trace, only to show up again in the middle of the night without saying anything to you?"

"I don't know. Maybe I was too happy he was back home again, where he belonged; I just forgot to ask him about it."

Dr. Lisa started writing on her notepad, looking concerned. "Okay, continue on," she said.

The rest of the time James was on his business trip seemed to go by fast, especially when I didn't want him to come home. I wanted him gone forever. I dreaded him walking through the door again. The thought of seeing him made me feel sick to my stomach. James being home meant I had to hide my relationship with Anthony, which I hated more than anything. It also meant I couldn't share a bed with the man I wanted to be with and loved more than life itself.

The day that James came home was the same day Anthony finished the large planter box I wanted him to build. I was in the house cleaning up, making the beds, picking up my clothes I left lying around the house and making sure there wasn't anything out of place that would give James any suspicion about what was going on with Anthony and I.

I went over to the window and saw Anthony standing next to his completed project out in the yard, looking it over and admiring his work. I knocked on the window to get his attention. When he looked over, I gave him a wave and blew him a kiss. He blew one back and then waved at me with his arm, signaling me to go out to him.

As I was walking in his direction, I couldn't help but notice his beauty. He was so handsome, standing there with sweat dripping from his brow and the sunlight beating down onto his shirtless body.

He looked at me and asked, "So, what do you think, my sexy lady?"

I leaned into his shoulder, staring at what he had just built. "It's wonderful. It's big enough, which is what I wanted. I should be able to get a few good rows of veggies growing in this. You did a great job."

"Thank you, Cindy. Now it just needs to be filled with dirt and you're ready to plant. We can use the old pile of dirt next to the greenhouse, but we will have to get something to fertilize it with. The manure pile isn't quite ready yet," he said.

"Gotcha. Fertilizer. Dirt."

"Okay, beautiful. I'm going to take a quick shower to rinse this sweat off of me and cool off."

I opened my mouth, stuck my fingertip on my tongue and pressed it on his chest while making a hissing sound. "You better go and do that because you are very hot, my sexy carpenter. If James weren't coming home today, I would get in the shower with you right now."

He smiled and went off to take his shower.

I no longer felt any guilt or shame about my affair with Anthony. It felt empowering. I loved everything about our relationship. The way I see it, it was James that pushed me into the arms of Anthony. I didn't ask for any of this. It is James's fault. When he treated me well and gave me the attention I needed,

I never even noticed other good-looking men. I always stayed focused on him. It's crazy how fast a relationship can crumble and how quickly you can fall out of love with a person when they show no interest in you.

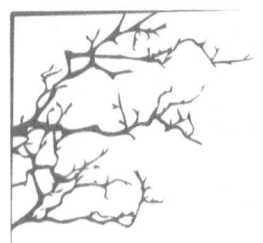

Chapter 7

Later, Anthony and I were sitting on the couch in the living room when my phone rang. It was James. I put it on speakerphone and said "hello."

"Hi, love. I just wanted to let you know I will be home later. I was wondering if you wanted to go out with me tonight. We can go grab a bite to eat at our favorite restaurant. I know we have spent no time together since we moved into the new house and I feel bad about it," he said.

"Um, I'm not in the mood. It's been a long day," I said.

Anthony pointed at me and started shaking his head up and down. He started waving his hand at me and pointing to the door.

"Okay, James, I guess I will go with you."

"That's great. I will see you when I get home," he said. Then he hung up.

"Why did you do that, Anthony? You know I didn't want to go with him."

"Because you always complained before about him not spending time with you. If you turn him down now, especially after all the time we spend together, then he is going to think something is going on between us. Just go out with him. It's only dinner."

"Okay, I will go have dinner with him...but only dinner. If he tries anything with me...I will cut his dick off."

When James got home, he found me sitting on the couch, in a trance again. "Cindy. Are you okay? Cindy?"

"Oh, hi James. Sorry, I must have been daydreaming."

"Cindy, I'm getting worried about you. You haven't been acting like yourself and this thing with you being in some kind of weird trance has me concerned. Maybe you should talk to someone. Like a counselor or even a therapist, if you prefer."

"You think I need a shrink? Are you kidding me right now?"

"I just think you need to talk to someone to find out what's going on," he said.

"You think you know what I need? The one person who is never around. The guy that has spent our whole marriage keeping me in this house alone? That guy? He thinks I need therapy? I can go to therapy, if that's what you want, and let whoever it is know you're the reason I need therapy, and then they will want to talk to you as well. Can you fit that into your busy schedule, James?"

"Okay, I'm sorry. I didn't want to upset you," he said.

"Too late for that, James."

"I'm going to go get changed. See you in a few minutes?"

"It's not like I can go anywhere, James."

He leaned down and tried to give me a kiss. I turned my head to the side to avoid it. While he went to get changed, I went down the hall and opened Anthony's door. He was lying back on his bed and watching t.v.

"I'm going to beat you for making me do this," I said.

"Don't threaten me with a good time!" he replied.

I giggled and then stuck my tongue out at him before I said, "Be careful what you wish for."

Then I heard James yell from the living room, "Cindy! Are you ready to go?" I took one last look at Anthony and said, "I have to go, troublemaker. See you in the morning." I walked down the hall to meet up with James. He looked me dead in the face and asked, "Who were you talking to?"

"Oh, no one," I told him.

We got into the car and went to dinner. We didn't talk the whole ride there. Or, maybe, I'm the one who didn't do any talking. James tried to strike up conversations with me, but I just ignored him. I wasn't ready to talk to him. He doesn't understand. He has made me emotionally unavailable to him. As long as I have Anthony, it's never going to change.

Dinner was just as awkward as the car ride. We talked little, other than the few words exchanged about the menu or what wine we wanted. The whole thing was a waste of time. I mean, what the hell was he thinking? Did he think that one night out to dinner was going to make up for everything he has put me through?

When we got home, he jumped into the shower. His suitcase was lying on the bed and I felt bad for some stupid reason. He took me out to dinner. That's the most he has done for me since we moved in here. I figured I could at least put his clothes away for him, so he didn't have to deal with it himself. I unzipped his suitcase and opened it up. "What the hell?" His dirty clothes smelled like women's perfume and his business clothes remained untouched. I smelled this perfume once before, but I can't remember where. I heard the shower shut off. My temper was flaring at this point. I flung his suitcase on to the floor and it made a big thud.

James stepped out of the shower and into the doorway. "Is everything alright, Cindy?"

I picked up a book that was sitting on the dresser and flung it at his head. It missed, and it hit the wall next to him. "Ugh!" I screamed out of pure frustration.

His eyes darkened. "Cindy, I think you should start sleeping on the couch from now on. The last thing I need right now is to be sleeping in bed at night, next to a psycho."

I couldn't believe what I just heard. The nerve of him. He is kicking me out of our bedroom and punishing me by making me sleep on the couch? I wish the book would have hit him right in the face. I grabbed my pillow and then stomped out of the room, slamming the door. I heard him yell through the door, "You know what your problem is, Cindy? You're fucked in the head!"

The next morning, James was already back at work. Actually, I'm not sure if he had to work that day or if he was keeping away from me. I can't remember. I was busy with my daily morning routine when my phone rang. It was Vicky.

"Hey, girlfriend. How are you?"

"Hi, Vicky, I'm fine. Why do you ask?"

"Okay, Cindy, promise not to get mad at me."

"I won't, but if you don't hurry and tell me, I promise I will get mad."

"James called me this morning. He wanted me to call you because he is concerned about you. He told me you've been acting strange, talking to yourself, and spacing out. Also, he said you flipped out on him last night and threw a book at him?"

"I flipped out because when I went to unpack his suitcase, like a good little wife, his clothes smelled like perfume and he never even wore his business attire."

"Cindy, did you ask him about it, or did you go through his suitcase?"

"No, Vicky, I just flipped out. I'm so sick of his bullshit."

"Hey, girl, don't jump to any conclusions right away. I mean, how do you know he didn't buy you a bottle of perfume on his trip to give you as a gift? You should have checked."

"I don't know. It's not like him to buy me gifts. The only thing he has given me since we got married is a life of solitude and heartache."

"Well sweetie, if he bought you perfume, you can count on one thing."

"What's that, Vicky?"

"That the bottle of perfume is now sitting in the trash somewhere."

"What about his business clothes, Vicky? He never wore them."

"Cindy, who knows? Maybe this trip was more of a casual trip. It could have been just a bunch of guys discussing business at some resort. Or maybe he did his work on his laptop, in his hotel room. He might just need his suit with him in case he has a meeting or something."

"I guess that could be the case, Vicky, but I don't know. I've got a bad feeling about it. It would anger me so much to know that some other woman is the reason he hasn't been around our whole marriage, and the reason I've been rotting in this house all this time. Did he bother to tell you he kicked me out of the bedroom and told me to sleep on the couch from now on?"

Vicky's tone changed. "He did what to you?"

"Yes, he kicked me out of the bedroom. He called me a psycho and told me I am fucked in the head. I don't even care. I hate him so much I don't want to sleep next to him, anyway."

"Yeah, but the couch, Cindy? What a dick! He must be punishing you. You should just stay in the other bedroom."

"We both know how much I would love to stay in the other bedroom. James wouldn't like it very much. He has to act like my boss, flex his authority over me, and exile me to the couch to feel like he's in control. He told me to sleep on the couch, so that is what I am going to do. I'm going to show him how happy I am being on the couch without him, just to drive him mad."

"Listen, Cindy, can you promise me you'll be on your best behavior from here on out so I can call him and get him off my back?"

"No promises, Vicky, but I will try."

"Good enough for me," she said.

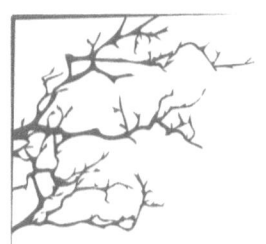

Chapter 8

I went outside to find Anthony and to see what he was up to. As I was walking by the barn, I could hear him on the phone. I started getting nosey and stopped to listen in on his call.

"Yeah, things are fine. I miss you too. Once winter is over up there, I will be back home sooner than you know. Okay. Love you too. Bye."

What the fuck was that? And who the hell was he talking to? After dealing with James's shit last night, this is what I walk out to today? I'm going to snap and have a nervous breakdown. Is he seeing someone else and hiding it from me, too? Can my life get any worse right now? I stormed into the barn and confronted him.

"Anthony, who was that?"

He said, "That was Brenda, a girlfriend back home.".

I snapped at him. "You never mentioned her to me."

With a stern look on his face, he said, "I never saw the point of telling you. What does it matter anyway? You know James hired me on a temporary basis. Once all the projects are done, he will let me go."

"Anthony, it would have been nice to know, while we are having sex, you have a girlfriend."

"Cindy, you are married. Let's not forget about that."

I realized he was right. "Okay, that's a fair point." I mean, I knew he was right, but it hurt to know he was going back to someone else while I wanted him all to myself. I need to get rid of James. If I can just get rid of James, then Anthony can move in permanently and we can be together forever.

After about a week went by, I was almost over Brenda, for now, whoever she was. Although she crosses my mind every single day.

I woke up to the sound of James leaving for work. Most things would wake me up as I didn't sleep great on the couch where I was still spending my nights. I think he relished it because he could exercise his authority over me and force me to sleep on the couch as punishment for standing up to him or not behaving like his good little servant. All I am to James anymore is just a possession.

Some mornings, on his way out the door, James would cover me back up with the blanket before he left. I still slept in the nude, and it bothered James that I was sleeping on our couch like that. I've slept nude almost my whole life. Wearing clothes in bed was too uncomfortable for me and caused sleepless nights of tossing and turning. Not to mention the couch was already uncomfortable enough. The only comfort I had being on the couch was staring down the hall at Anthony's bedroom door. I was always hoping he would come out for something and see me lying here naked so I could tease him.

With Anthony right down the hall and big open picture windows lining the porch wall across from the couch, the last thing James wanted was me sleeping naked. If James only knew that Anthony already knows every square inch of my body, inside and out. Or if he knew the things he was doing to his wife every day, while he was away, being naked on the couch would be the least of his concerns.

One night, a fight started between us over it. I was getting ready to go to bed and James said, "Why don't you try keeping some clothes on for a change? Nobody wants to see you naked. What's next? You, walking around the house like that and acting like a fucking whore?"

I felt my face get flush. What did he just say to me? I could feel my blood boiling. I tried to bite my tongue but couldn't. "For one, James, you're the only person who doesn't care to see me naked. For two, thanks for the idea of walking around the house that way. I just might do that. And three, I would rather be someone's whore than be your wife! Now if you don't mind, I am going to bed, on the couch, right where you want your psycho wife."

Standing right in front of him, I undressed and threw my clothes all over the floor. I jumped onto the couch naked and laid down on top of the blanket. I placed my hands behind my head on the pillow, turned, looked at him with a smile and said, "Goodnight, James." His face got bright red with anger. He stormed down the hall to the bedroom and slammed the door so hard it shook the house.

The following day, when I made my morning visit to Anthony's room, I found him lying awake, waiting for his alarm to go off. He took one long look at me standing there, without a single article of clothing on, and said, "I like what I see."

"Move over a little," I told him.

He slid over and propped himself up on his side. I climbed up next to him, got on my side and snuggled my back right up to him. I grabbed his arm and pulled it over me. As soon as I got comfortable, his phone rang. He picked up his phone, looked at me, and said, "Shh."

To my disappointment, Brenda was calling his phone. I couldn't believe it. I never see him talking on the phone, other than the one time the other day and the time he mentioned a hot little blonde to someone. And this bitch has to be calling now? Right when I climbed into bed with him? I could feel the jealousy and anger growing inside of me. If she were here right now, I would strangle her. I whispered to him as he answered the phone, "Real fucking nice, Anthony."

He seemed calm and unfazed by my rude comment while he put the phone to his ear. "Hey, Brenda. How are you? No, you didn't wake me. I've been awake, just lying here in bed. No, it's fine that you called."

I refused to deal with his behavior. I got myself up out of the bed and gave him a look of disgust. He shrugged his shoulders at me while I walked out of the room.

The rest of the day was a struggle for me because I couldn't get Brenda out of my head now. What am I going to do about her? I wanted Anthony all to myself. I am falling for him hard and I love him. The thought of him going back to her made me want to cry. Thinking about her putting her hands on him made me feel sick. Or worse, her making love to him. I need to put a stop to this. I can't let her take him away from me when I'm in love and happy again. She must not get in the way.

Throughout the day, Anthony could tell something was bothering me. He kept asking me if I was okay and I just kept ignoring him. As the day started ending, he walked over to me, brushed my hair away from my face and asked again.

I leaned into him, gave him a kiss, and reassured him. "Yes, everything is fine." But I know, deep down inside, everything is not fine.

Dr. Lisa interjected, "Let me ask you something."

I responded, "Sure,"

"Cindy, I'm trying to wrap my head around what's going on here and make sense of it. Maybe you can clear up some of my confusion?"

"Okay," I said.

"When you were young, you had an imaginary friend named Brenda to fill the void in your life. You created her to deal with the stress and anxiety of being alone all the time and to bring you comfort when you were being bullied in school. I guess what I'm trying to ask is... is this Brenda a made up person also?"

"Oh my gosh, no. She is real. I'm not a child anymore and I'm a little too old to be making up imaginary people."

Dr. Lisa gave me a puzzled look and tapped her pen on her notepad a couple of times. "It's my job to ask these questions and get a sense of what's going on. You're at a point where you are really falling in love with Anthony and you're already seeing your husband as a threat to your relationship with him. I'm just wondering if your mind has brought back Brenda again, only this time as a threat, so you can get rid of her for good? Now that you have Anthony, you no longer need Brenda or your husband?"

"What? No, that's ridiculous. Like I said, I'm not a child anymore."

"I understand what you're saying, Cindy, but also understand that, yes, these things can be just a childhood phase someone goes through and they at some point get over it, but also, these things sometimes carry over into adulthood and don't reappear until certain triggers bring it back. I'm having a hard time believing it's a coincidence that both girls are named Brenda."

I yelled at Dr. Lisa, "I already told you she is real! It's all real! Why don't you just listen to me and stop treating me like I'm crazy!"

"Okay, calm down Cindy. Just relax and take a deep breath. You're getting emotional. Why don't we wrap this up today and I can come back tomorrow," she said. Then she got up out of the chair and started heading for the door.

I screamed as she walked out of the room, "Here's an idea, Doc! You can just leave me alone and never come back here again!"

What the hell is wrong with everyone? These people are ridiculous. Why are they all treating me like I'm crazy? I didn't ask for any of this. Why are James and Vicky lying about Anthony? Why can't they just tell the truth so I can get out of here? I didn't ask to be neglected and left alone or ask to get a head injury. James is the one who recommended hiring Anthony and suggested he stay with us. The only thing I'm guilty of is falling in love with someone other than my husband after he abandoned me.

I laid here crying and soon fell asleep. I'm not sure how long I was asleep for when a tapping noise woke me up. I looked over, and it was Anthony standing in the hall tapping on the glass. He looked very shaken up. His facial expression was a look of dismay. I could tell something was very wrong. I reached my arms out and called to him, "Baby, come here. I need you. Oh my gosh, I need you, Anthony."

He looked over his shoulder and then back at me. I watched his lips move as he spoke the words "I love you" through the glass just before he ran off.

"No, baby, come back. Please, baby. Don't leave me. Please come back Anthony," I yelled. I started crying. This time, it wasn't a nightmare. It was real. Anthony was standing outside of my room. Why did he not come in to see me? Why did he just run off like that?

Then, out of the corner of my eye, I saw the door open. I looked up, and to my disappointment, it was James.

"Who are you yelling at, and why are you crying, Cindy?"

"James, what the hell are you doing here?"

"I thought I would stop by to see how you are doing?"

"James, I don't want to see you. Get out! You're a lying fucking bastard! Do you hear me? A lying bastard! Don't come back!"

He squinted his eyes as he gave me an evil stare. He started to open his mouth, as if to say something, then he turned and headed to the door. As he walked out of the room, the nurse came in. She could tell I was crying and upset about something. She handed me the box of tissues from the bedside table.

"Cindy, are you okay?"

"I will be okay as long as James doesn't come back. He ruined my chance to see Anthony."

"Who?" she asked.

"Anthony. The man that was standing outside of my room a few minutes ago."

She looked shocked by what I told her. "I've been sitting at the nurse's station the whole time and I saw no one standing there, doll."

"Really? If you didn't see Anthony standing there, then you weren't paying any attention to what was going on around you."

"Okay, let's get something to help you relax. I will be back in a minute," she said.

The nurse came back in and gave me some medication. The rest of the night was one big blur from there on out. I just laid in bed, comfortable, with nothing on my mind and not a care in the world. I slept all night long without waking up through the night.

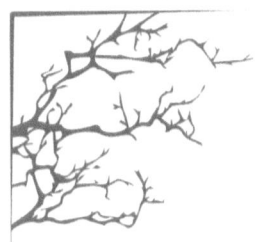

Chapter 9

"Good morning, Cindy. Are we feeling better today?"

"Yes, Dr. Lisa. I saw him yesterday."

"Whom was it you seen?" she asked, eagerly awaiting my answer.

"I saw Anthony. He was standing outside of my room, looking in, until James scared him off."

Dr. Lisa looked unfazed by what I just told her. "Ah, yes, Anthony. The nurse told me about it on my way in. And nobody else saw Anthony standing outside of your room? I want you to think about that for a minute, Cindy."

I started to get annoyed. "No, it's not my fault they don't pay any attention to what goes on around here. I mean, what's next? They don't see James in my room when he comes back to kill me?"

She pushed her glasses further up her nose while continuing to write on her notepad. "Why would you think your husband would try to kill you?"

"Have you met the asshole? Never mind, I don't want to talk about it." I turned my head in the opposite direction and crossed my arms, hoping she would go away.

"Cindy, do you feel comfortable about starting where we left off yesterday? If at any point you feel uncomfortable, or feel yourself becoming agitated, just let me know and we can talk about something else."

"Okay, Dr. Lisa. It's pretty apparent I don't have a choice in the matter. Um, where was I? Oh yeah, I remember."

I heard Anthony say, "Baby, get up," as he was nudging my arm.

I asked, almost unable to open my eyes, "What time is it?"

"Time to get your sexy ass out of bed and go on a trail ride with me." He ripped the blanket off of me, exposing me, and said in a silly tone, mocking James, "Why don't you try keeping some clothes on for a change?" I slapped him on the side of the leg while still trying to wake up.

"What!" he said, smiling. "You don't think I heard you two arguing the other night? My door is right down the hall. And... for you... clothing is optional. I am loving what I see right now."

I put my hand on his inner thigh. "That's funny because I feel like clothing isn't an option when I'm around you, bad boy."

"Don't start, Cindy, or we will never make it on our trail ride in time. On a serious note, though, I'm sorry you had to put up with that from him. He was way out of line with his comments to you. As soon as I heard him throw the 'whore' word at you, I got so mad, I got out of bed and put my pants on to go confront him. Actually, I'm lying. I was on my way out to beat the shit out of him, honestly."

"What stopped you?" I asked.

"I was on my way to the door and I remembered... nevermind, it's not important. Come on, get your sexy ass up. The horses are ready and waiting."

I jumped up from the couch and ran to my room. I threw on a pair of jeans, a light tank top, my favorite western boots and hat, then went outside to meet up with Anthony.

It was such a gorgeous day. The sun was shining. It was about 80 degrees, with a slight breeze. The sky was bright blue with only a couple of white puffy clouds hanging off in the distance. The miles of green pasture swayed in the breeze. It was a perfect day for a ride. We got up onto the horses and headed out into the rolling hills.

I turned and looked at Anthony. "This is fun and I'm sure the horses are loving it, too. They've been needing some exercise," I said.

Anthony looked over at me and nodded his head in agreement. "Hey Cindy, can I ask you something?"

"Sure, anything. What is it?"

"I know your marriage with James isn't doing well and I've noticed it getting worse and worse. Is it because of our relationship together? Am I getting in the way of your marriage to James?"

"Oh my gosh, Anthony, no. Please don't think that at all. Our marriage crumbled when we moved here to the farm. You know how much he works. He is never around. I was home alone and going out of my mind. It was driving me crazy. That and the fact he refused to help me with anything around here. He is always too tired on his days off or just doesn't care to help. We haven't had sex forever. He just ignores and neglects me. It has caused a lot of arguments between James and I. We drifted apart long before you got here."

He then asked me, "Do you think he's having an affair?"

I thought for a second. "It never crossed my mind before, but at this point, it wouldn't surprise me if he is."

Anthony looked at me and winked. "So that's why you hired me. I get it now. You hired me to be the man he can't be," he said.

"Oh, you're more of a man than he could ever be," I said.

He lifted his arms and started playfully flexing them and showing off, "It also helps to have better muscles too," he replied.

I giggled and said, "That's not the only thing better on you."

"Cindy, you better be careful with your choice of words. Don't you know what flirting and compliments will get you?"

"I don't know. Why don't you tell me? What will it get me?"

He smiled at me and said, "I guess you will have to catch me to find out." Then he took off running across the field. I braced my legs on the side of my horse, hunched down, and went chasing after him. By the time I caught up with him, he was already off his horse, standing there, waiting for me. He walked over and helped me get down.

"It's about time you got here. I was getting ready to send out the search party."

"Ha ha, Anthony. You're such a smartass. It's one of the many reasons I'm so in love with you." I then realized what I said. I felt embarrassed. It just slipped out. I can't even imagine what is going through his mind right now. I don't want to scare him off. Why am I so stupid and why did I say such a dumb thing? "I'm so sorry Anthony, I... I didn't mean to..."

He cut me off. "How about we let the horses graze for a little and go sit in the grass together?"

"Um, yeah. Okay, sounds good," I said.

We sat for a little while, silent and staring out over the hills.

"Isn't this wonderful, Anthony? It's so beautiful and it's such a perfect day."

"I agree," he said.

"Anthony, can we talk about something without you getting upset with me?"

He turned and looked at me. "Sure," he said.

"What's the deal with Brenda? Have the two of you been together long? Are you in love with her? I don't mean to pry, but it's been bothering me quite a bit."

He placed his hand on my knee. "I've known Brenda for a long time. It has always been a kind of complicated situation with her and I. We dated years ago and then we were on and off for a while. We both soon realized we were better off as friends, so we broke it off but continued having sex with each other sometimes, in between dating and relationships. We share an apartment to ease rent costs, but we do each have our own bedrooms."

"Yeah, but you said 'Love you' to her on the phone and you also said the two of you have sex?"

"I say 'Love You' to her in the same way I would say it to a sister. It's something that we have always said to each other. I'm not in love with her, the same way that you're not in love with James. As far as sex, we haven't been in bed together for quite some time and we have no intentions of sleeping together again."

I looked him in the eyes and said, "I feel a little better, but I still... oh, never mind. You wouldn't understand."

"Cindy, I understand more than you know. Would you like to know how I understand?"

"Yes, I would love to know."

"I understand because I'm in love with you, too."

I started bursting with excitement and almost started to shake and cry with pure bliss. I held back my tears of joy and jumped on top of him, pushing him down onto his back. I kissed him like I would never see him again, and he returned the kiss with just as much passion. He kissed me like he cherished me and like there was nothing else in the world that mattered to him at this very moment.

We laid on the ground, staring into each other's eyes, while he played with my hair. There was no reason to talk or say a single word to each other. Our gaze said it all. Anthony turned his head toward the sky to see the position of the sun. "We should start heading back just in case James comes home. We can't be too careful," he said.

He seemed a little too paranoid and concerned about James, judging by his expression. It puzzled me. I said, "I'm not worried about James. He couldn't hurt a fly. Why do you seem so worried about him, Anthony?"

"Cindy, I need to tell you something, and you need to swear it stays between us."

"I swear," I said

"When you started sleeping on the couch, he confronted me one day. He pulled me aside, backed me into a wall, and put a gun to my chest. A gun, Cindy! He told me that if he ever finds out I touched his wife, he would kill me and bury my body where no one will ever find it. He wasn't joking, and he was as serious as a person can be. The blank stare in his eyes freaked me out. It was like his eyes turned black and he was staring right through me. It was very unnerving. You need to be careful. James isn't who you think he is. He is very dangerous."

I didn't know what to think of what Anthony just told me. It doesn't sound like James, but then again, his outbursts and comments toward me lately aren't like him either.

"Come on, Cindy. We should get back."

We got on our horses and headed back to the house.

That night when James got home, he just walked right past me in the living room. He didn't look at me or say anything to me. In fact, he didn't even acknowledge I was there. He just walked right to the bedroom and closed the door behind him.

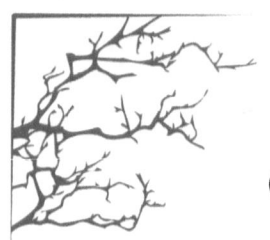

Chapter 10

As the week went on, I started to be a little more cautious around James. I still didn't know what to think about everything. The perfume smell that radiated from his clothes in the suitcase, the way he's been talking to me, his temper, all the late nights of coming home and going straight to bed. Then there's the thing he did to Anthony with a gun. Why would he threaten him with a gun? What is going on? I wondered.

Any time I'm around James now, I feel uneasy. I'm more aware of his actions and behavior. I'm focused on his unusual demeanor. Any new little quirk he has or change in his attitude annoyed me and got my radar up. I'm at the point I can't even stand the sound of his voice or the way he walks. Everything about him makes my anger boil to the surface. These are things I never noticed about James before. Did I not see all of his imperfections early on because I was in love with him? Maybe we got married too soon and too young? Come to think of it, we never had an intimate relationship where we got to know each other well. We were just young adults making quick irrational decisions about our lives.

When I think of him threatening Anthony, anger takes over my mind and then paranoia soon sets in. Would he kill Anthony if he found out about us? Then what's next? He would have to kill me too, because I would never let him get away with it. If he ever hurt my precious Anthony, my angry face would be the last thing he ever saw again. Or maybe he plans on killing us both if he found out about us. He would almost have to, or he would risk getting caught because I would turn him in myself if I don't get the chance to kill him first. I need to protect Anthony. I will get the handgun from the closet and keep it under the couch pillow, just in case. If James finds out it's missing, I can tell him I have it because the front door is right across from where I sleep. He will understand I want to feel safe from any unwanted intruders. At least, I think he would.

I went to the closet, opened the door, and turned the light on. His hunting rifle was leaning up against the wall where it has always been, and on the shelf is the gun case that housed the handgun I wanted to take. I stood there and opened the case. What I saw shocked me, or should I say, what I didn't see? "What? Why is it missing and where the hell is it?" I looked on the shelves and checked everywhere in the closet, but couldn't find it. That means James has it. Why would he have it? Does he plan on doing something with it? This is not good. Anthony must be telling the truth about James threatening him with a gun. I shut off the light and closed the door. I had to go find Anthony and warn him it's missing.

"Anthony! I have to tell you something."

"What's wrong, Cindy? You look worried."

I was almost completely frantic when I told him. "I went in the closet to get the handgun and it's gone. It's really gone. That means James has it. Why would he have it? Why? Do you think he's planning something? I don't trust him, especially with the way he's been acting. He must be planning on shooting us. That's the only thing I can think of. He is going to kill us! Yup, he's definitely going to kill us, Anthony. What are we going to do about it?"

"Cindy, calm down," he said. Then he pulled me against his chest and held me. "You are panicking for no reason. He works in town and he doesn't leave until late, most nights. I'm sure he keeps it with himself for protection. I would do the same thing if I were him."

Anthony could always calm me down. "You're probably right, but I still don't trust him."

"I don't trust him either, but let's not get crazy and jump to conclusions."

"Okay, I love you, Anthony."

"I love you too, baby girl. Why don't you go relax with a book or watch some television to get your mind off of things?"

I went back inside and made my way to the bedroom closet, where I had a stack of books up on the shelf I never read. I reached up and grabbed one. This should get my mind off of things for a little while, I thought.

I snuggled into my spot on the couch underneath my blanket. "Okay, what's this book about? I turned it over. Let's see. Suspenseful. Edge of your seat thriller. I continued on... What? The wife disappears! They suspect the husband did it! Okay, this will not help me right now. Reading is not an option."

I threw the book on the end table, laid down and tried to take a nap. As soon as I got comfortable, my mind started drifting, and I fell asleep. When I woke, it was dark, and I wondered what time it was. I looked over at the clock on the wall. 7:00 p.m. I better call James and let him know there won't be any dinner tonight.

"Cindy, what's up?" James said, answering his phone.

"I wanted to let you know there's no dinner tonight. I laid down and ended up falling asleep. Get something before you head home." Before he responded, I heard the faint voice of another woman in the background. She giggled and said "James, come here" with a long soft draw. Then there was a long pause before she giggled again.

"James, are you there?"

"Yeah, sorry. I'm a little caught up in something right now. Don't worry about it, I already ate. It's going to be another long night at the office. I won't be home before eleven tonight."

"Okay," I said, and we hung up.

My curiosity got the best of me. Who was that in the background? I got up and ran to Anthony's room. He was laying there watching t.v. when I barged through the door.

"Hey, what's up?" he asked.

"Remember when you asked me if I thought James was having an affair?"

"Yes, what about it?"

"Well, I called to let him know I fell asleep and didn't make any dinner, and I heard another woman in the background. He seemed very preoccupied with her. I heard her giggle at him and say his name. What I don't get about the whole situation is why would he threaten you if he's been seeing somebody all along?"

"Maybe your husband is the jealous kind. You know, the ones who say 'I don't want her, but you can't have her,' type."

"Maybe you're right. Have a good night's sleep. I will see you in the morning. I love you."

"I love you too, Cindy."

I went into the living room and turned on the lamp next to the couch. Everything was so exhausting at this point that I just wanted to lie down again. I got undressed and got back under my blanket. I couldn't understand what I did to deserve all of this. Why would he buy me a house in the country and marry me if he was cheating on me? This explains why, after our marriage, he was always home late and refused to have sex with me. Why would he marry me only to destroy me? And to top it off, he threatens Anthony not to touch his wife. I don't understand. Does he get pleasure from treating me like his possession?

Then I thought about Anthony. I'm so happy I have him. I don't know what I would do without him and to think that my piece of shit husband threatened him with a gun? He's sleeping with another woman and he has the balls to threaten Anthony, saying he would kill him if he touched me. Again, he's the one that pushed me to Anthony! But if I try to divorce James, he will kill me. He knows I would get the house in the divorce and I know he would never allow me to take anything he sees as belonging to him. Especially something he works and pays for. There's only one way out of this. James needs to die.

After a few hours had gone by, he came walking through the front door. "You're still awake, Cindy? Oh yeah, I forgot you took a nap today. Sorry I'm home so late. I really had my hands full at work. I'm completely drained."

"I can only imagine, James," I said.

Then he went straight to the bedroom and shut the door. After he went to his room, a faint smell of perfume lingered in the air. It smelled familiar to me, but I still couldn't figure out where I smelled it before. Then I heard the shower start.

Dr. Lisa interjected. "When you found out about James threatening Anthony, is that around the time your paranoia started?" she asked.

"Yes, it got worse when I realized he was having his own affair because I was the only thing standing in his way. I was living in the house I wanted to be in. He knows I won't give it up so easily. He also knows I have a strong case for divorce. What judge would give a man a home he is never at, while taking it away from the one person who is always there? And if I can prove his affair has been going on our whole marriage, I will not only get the house, he will work his ass off to pay me alimony as well. So, to answer your question, yes, I was getting paranoid."

"Was James aware of your suspicions?"

"No, if I dared to tell him or if he found out, I knew he would kill me right away, and I'm not the only one who is concerned about James."

"Anthony and I went away for a weekend once, and I swear James was stalking us. As a matter of fact, I swear to this day it was him."

"Tell me about it," she said.

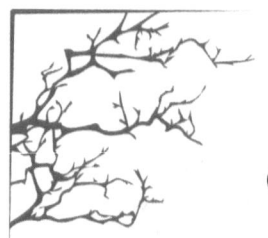

Chapter 11

It was Anthony's idea to go away. We were sitting on the back porch eating dinner when he told me.

I remember I yelled across the house, "Dinner is done, James. Do you want to eat out on the back porch with us, or do you want to eat in your office?"

He yelled back, "I'll just take my plate in here. I'm heading to bed soon anyway, and I don't feel like getting up right now." I made all our plates, brought James's plate down to him, and went out on the back porch to eat with Anthony.

"This is delicious. Thank you, Cindy," Anthony said.

"You're welcome."

Anthony leaned over the table and in a soft voice, said, "I've been thinking about something."

My eyes widened at the way he was being discreet. "Thinking about what?" I asked.

"There's this place I saw once while I was traveling. It's three hours north of here. It's a country style hotel. I was going to spend a night there once, but I didn't want to pay the cost. The rooms are like small, luxurious apartments. There's a Jacuzzi in every room. They also have an enormous pool and hot tub outside. The town is delightful, too. It's a small town. It has an exceptional little diner that serves good food. There's a small pond with row boats you can rent and there's even a drive-in movie theater."

"It sounds like a nice place," I said.

"It is, and the reason I'm telling you is, I think we should go."

I leaned across the table. "What? When? How can we go?"

He swallowed another bite of his food. "This weekend, after James leaves, we can go. He leaves Friday night. We can get up early on Saturday morning and head out. We will check into our room, then go have lunch at the Diner and check out the town. The following day we can hang out by the pool, go for a boat ride or do whatever you want. Then Monday morning, we can head back. It will be perfect. What do you think?"

"It sounds amazing. Let's do it," I said.

After James left Friday night for his work trip. Anthony and I each packed a bag so we would be ready in the morning. We were both excited. This is going to be our first real vacation together. We won't have to hide our relationship around town. No one is going to know who we are that far away.

If I didn't spend that Friday night snuggled into Anthony's warm body after James left, I wouldn't have gotten any sleep. I was so excited to go on our first trip together. We got up early and hit the road. We stopped for donuts and coffee before we started making the drive. About halfway into our drive, we made another stop for fuel and water, then continued on our way.

"Hey, Anthony."

"Yes, baby."

"Do you see the red car a ways back from us?"

"Yeah, what about it, my love?"

"Well, it's been following us most of the way and I thought nothing of it until now. When we stopped at the gas station, the same car pulled in and parked on the other side of the lot. What was strange about it, is nobody ever got out of the car. They just sat there. Once we started driving again, it followed us and has been following us ever since."

"Maybe it's just a coincidence, Cindy. We can at least say it's not James. The car behind us is red and James's car is black."

"Yeah, I guess you're right."

"So, gorgeous, are you getting hungry? I figured we can hit that diner for some brunch before we check in. I'm not sure I can wait until after check-in. What do you say? Cindy? Baby? Are you okay?"

"Oh, I'm so sorry, Anthony. I was watching the car and zoned out, I guess. What were you saying?"

"Are you hungry?"

"Yes, I could use something to eat."

We pulled into the Diner when we got to town. It was cute. It reminded me of an enormous Airstream camper. Stainless steel covered the whole outside of the building. The inside was red and yellow, with matching booths. There was even a jukebox in the corner playing music. There weren't many people inside. Just a few locals, I assume. We got a booth at the front side of the Diner, next to the window. The server took our order. I opted for breakfast, and Anthony got a burger and fries. We were in the middle of eating, when I noticed out the window, the red car sitting across the street from us.

"Look Anthony, it's that car again."

"Where, Cindy?"

"Over there, parked across the street, facing us."

"Let's finish up here and head to the hotel."

"Anthony, what if it follows us?"

"If it does, I will drive a different way there. I can take some side streets to lose them if they follow us."

"Okay," I said.

We left the Diner and started heading to the hotel to check in. Anthony took a bunch of side roads and went in different directions, just in case we were being followed.

"I'm going to park somewhere out of sight and go check in while you wait in the car. Once I get our room key and I see the coast is clear, we can grab our bags and head in," he said.

We drove into the parking lot and found a spot off to the side, along the tree line, to park. Anthony went and got our room key and came back to get me. "I don't see that car anywhere, so we should be good," he said.

We grabbed our bags and went to our room. It was on the ground floor with one entrance door having access to the parking lot and another door on the other side of the room, which brought you out back to the pool and hot tub.

I still felt uneasy about the car that was following us, so we spent most of our time in the back by the pool, enjoying the sun all day.

Anthony turned to look at me and said, "Want to go get room service and then soak in the Jacuzzi for a little while before bed?"

"Sounds amazing. Let's do it."

We stepped back into our room and I noticed the front door was open about a foot. "What the hell? Anthony, did you leave the front door open?"

"No, I never touched it. Did you forget to close it?"

"No, I closed it and checked that it was closed. I might have forgotten to lock it, but I closed it. I'm sure I did. I even pulled on it. Can you please check the place and make sure that no one is hiding anywhere? I'm freaking out."

"Cindy, do you think housekeeping came by and forgot to close it?"

"Why would housekeeping come in when we just got here today? Oh shit! Look, the bathroom light is on. You know I'm not crazy now. I had you go back and shut it off after you changed."

"That, I know for a fact, Cindy. Someone has obviously been in here."

"Please go check around Anthony. I'm getting scared."

Anthony checked everywhere and didn't find anybody. Nothing of ours was missing, either. Once our nerves settled down, we ordered room service, locked the door, and ate while we sat in the Jacuzzi.

At bed time we were laying on the bed wrapped in nothing but a towel, talking. I needed something to get this day off of my mind. A distraction. I didn't want what happened today to ruin our weekend together.

I looked at Anthony and ran my finger down his chest. "I need something from you right now, please."

"What's that?" he asked.

"I want you to make love to me. Genuine love. Passionate love. Like I'm all yours and you're all mine.... like you could love no one as much as you love me. Can you do that for me?"

He placed his hand on my face, looked me right in the eye, and did just that.

The following morning, I woke up feeling so in love. I felt light on my feet, giddy, like I could fly. I could feel the romance in the air and I was head over heels for Anthony. Just when I think I can't fall more in love with him, it hits me like a wave and carries me deeper into ecstasy. I am so in love with him; I have butterflies in my stomach. I didn't feel this in love with James when he asked me to marry him, as emotional as it was for me. I feel like riding off into the sunset with Anthony to never return. He is my soulmate and I feel it deep down inside with every fiber of my being. I just know I belong with him and no one else.

Today is the beginning of a new life for me. I just know it is. Anthony and I always have great sex, but it's nothing like it was last night. How he made love to me was deep and emotional. I've felt nothing like it before in my life. The connection we had last night was so profound, the universe wouldn't have been able to pull us apart. He is mine and I am his forever. Nothing is going to bring me down today. Nothing.

I woke up thirsty from our long night. I wrapped my towel around my body so I could go to the ice machine and get some ice for my water. It was only a few doors down, inside a breezeway, alongside a couple of vending machines.

I opened the door and stepped out. Something across the parking lot caught my attention. "Oh, shit!" I said, while running back into the room and slamming the door shut behind me.

"Anthony, get up! Come on, get up!" I screamed.

"What's wrong?" he asked.

"Hurry and get dressed!"

"Why? What's happening, Cindy?"

"He's here, Anthony. He's fucking here!"

"Who's here?"

"James!"

"What?"

"Yeah, I was walking out of the room and I saw him standing across the parking lot, looking over at me. He was holding a gun in his hand. A gun, Anthony."

He buttoned up his pants, threw a shirt on, and went over to the window. He peeked out. "Where did you see him?"

I went over to show him. "He was standing over there."

"There's no one there," he said. "Are you sure it was James?"

"I'm pretty sure it was him. He was wearing a hat and sunglasses. It looked just like him. It has to be him. I know I'm not crazy. I know what I saw."

Anthony went to the door, leaned out, and started looking around. "I don't see him or his car anywhere. Cindy, he is on a work trip and we are three hours north of the house, in the opposite direction from town. Just calm down, baby. I think your mind is playing tricks on you."

"Yeah, maybe you're right." I couldn't help but think the worst. I was getting paranoid. Was that James? He looked so real. If it was, he now knows about Anthony and I. Did he come to hunt us down and kill us?

Anthony put his hand on my shoulder. "Baby?"

"Yes, handsome?"

"I know you're a little shook-up, so how about we leave today, instead of tomorrow, and head back home?"

"You would do that for me? Are you sure?"

"Of course. I couldn't live with myself, making you spend another night here after what you just went through. Let's pack up. I will load up the car and make sure no one is around, then we can head home."

I felt relieved to be back in the car and on our way back. We've been driving for thirty minutes now and still have two and a half hours to go before we get there. Time couldn't go by fast enough for me. I just wanted to get back. As I was thinking about home, I glanced at the side mirror and there it was again. The same red car that followed us on the way up, driving far enough back, and making it impossible to see who was driving.

"Anthony, look in the rear-view mirror. It's the same car again."

He looked up. "Shit, I think it is. I will pull off at the next exit, into a gas station, to see if it follows us."

As we approached the next exit, Anthony turned on his turn signal. I looked back and said, "They turned on theirs, too." At the last minute, Anthony merged back onto the highway, intentionally missing the exit ramp. I continued to watch the car behind us. "What the hell! They drove past the exit, as well."

"Okay, I'm getting off at the next exit and going to a gas station. If they follow us, at least we can find out who it is and what the hell it is they want. This is fucked up," he said.

Anthony pulled off of the highway, drove down the road a little ways to a busy gas station. About a minute later, the same red car drove past the gas station and kept on going.

"Could you see who was in the car, Anthony?".

"No, did you see who was in there?"

"No, but it looked like they were wearing a hat and glasses. It might be the same guy I saw standing in the parking lot."

He turned toward me and said, "Let's get back on the highway. It might just be a coincidence. It is pretty strange though, the same car which followed us on the way up is behind us again on the way back."

We got back on the highway and started heading home again. We were about half an hour from home and there was the car again, trailing behind us on the highway.

Anthony screamed, "What the hell!"

"What are we going to do, Anthony?"

"I'm going to get off the road up here and take a different way home. That way, if they follow us, I can lose them. Maybe we should go to the Sheriff's office and make a report?"

"Are you crazy? James is best friends with the Sheriff. How is that going to play out? Hi Ethan, my boyfriend and I snuck away to a hotel together, while James was out of town, and a car kept following us. Is that really what you want?"

"Okay, I get it. No police," he said.

We exited the highway and, to our surprise, the car kept going down the road.

"What a trip. What's next? We pull into the driveway together with our luggage and James is already home?"

"Please don't say that, Cindy. I'm not looking forward to getting shot today."

Thankfully, James wasn't home when we got there.

We spent the rest of the week living in paranoia over James and the car that kept following us. I kept wondering if James hired someone to spy on me and follow me around. I didn't understand why I thought I saw James when Anthony and I went away. Was I having hallucinations?

I kept looking out the windows, checking for anything or anyone. Every night I would go through the house, making sure I locked all the windows and doors. Anthony slept in the living room with me to ease my nerves and keep me calm. I gave him the couch while I slept curled up on the loveseat. I didn't want us to be at the end of the house, in his bedroom, and caught by surprise if someone came into the house in the middle of the night.

James came home the day he was due. He walked in acting like his usual self.

"How was your trip, James? Did anything exciting happen this week?" I asked.

"Nope, just the same old shit. A busy week of travel and work." That is all he said before he went down to bed with his plate of food that I left for him on the counter. He mentioned nothing about Anthony and I. Maybe I was seeing things when I thought it was him standing on the other side of the parking lot. Maybe I am going crazy?

It was strange that I felt at ease with James at home. I was feeling much more protected having two men in the house with me, even though the one I am married to is planning on killing me, or so I thought.

Dr. Lisa asked, "About that, Cindy. What makes you believe your husband would try to kill you?"

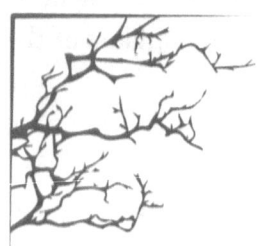

Chapter 12

Anthony told me one day about James's plan to kill us when he got home after a trip into town.

He said, "Cindy, we need to have a talk."

"Okay, right now?"

"Yes, right now."

"Anthony, you seem very worried. What is going on?"

"You're in a lot of danger, Cindy. We need to figure something out right away. I can't let this happen to you."

"Why am I in danger? Does it have something to do with the car that was following us?"

"No, it's James."

"Did he do something?"

"It's what he plans on doing, Cindy."

"You're worrying me, Anthony. Please tell me what is going on before I have a nervous breakdown."

He said, "On my way to town, I got a little drowsy. I fought it off, but I knew there would be no way I could make the drive back. I went to the lumberyard and got the materials I needed to put up the other section of fencing. Then I went over to the hardware store for some paint and a brush. On my way to the store, I could feel myself getting more and more tired, so

I thought I would go to the coffee shop and get a nice strong coffee before my trip back home."

"There wasn't any parking in front of the shop, so I parked on the side street, out of sight. I went in and ordered my coffee. Do you know the booths they have in the corner near the back? They have tall back rests for privacy?"

"Yes, I know the ones." I said.

"I sat in the very last one, back in the corner. I wasn't there for long before I heard James's voice. He was at the counter ordering his drink and he was with another woman."

"Who was the woman?"

"I don't know who she was. I had never seen her before."

"What did she look like?"

"Slender and fit with dark hair. She was about his height and age. I didn't want him to see me, especially since he was with this woman, so I put my head down and moved as close as I could to the wall. I left my coffee cup in view, so they thought the table was still dirty. At first I thought it might be someone he worked with and they were just getting coffee, but it was pretty obvious after their conversation they were more than what meets the eye. They sat in the booth right behind me. They didn't know I was there, so I sat still and stayed quiet so I could hear them talking. She started the conversation first."

"You need to do something soon, James. I will not wait around forever."

"Do something about what?"

"Your wife, Cindy. We've talked about this. When are you going to do something about her?"

"I don't know."

"You better figure something out soon. You and I have been seeing each other since college and she is going to find out one way or another. I'm surprised she hasn't figured it out yet."

"I doubt she will. I have her pretty convinced I'm taking work trips, so as long as she doesn't come by the office during the day or your place at night, things will be fine."

"That's not the point, James. Do you want to marry me or not?"

"That's a stupid question. You know I do."

"Do you honestly think she is going to let you have the house? It's her dream home. She is going to take it from you in the divorce and you're going to continue paying for a home you can't live in. On top of that, the bitch will make you pay her alimony as well. Do you want her taking everything you work so hard for?"

"No."

"Also, James, where are we going to live? I don't know about you, but I don't want to continue living in my apartment. Are you just going to let her stay in our home? You and I found that house together."

"Yes, it was supposed to be our house, but you didn't want to marry me then. I was going to dump Cindy for you, but you got cold feet and backed out. It was you I was supposed to marry, not her."

"That's your stupidity, James. You married her to teach me a lesson and look how that's worked out for you. Now you're stuck with a woman you don't love and who is living in our home. She is your mistake and your problem. Now you have to do something about it."

"And what would you like me to do?"

"Oh my gosh, James! You're such an idiot sometimes. Do I have to spell it out for you? Get rid of her. I don't care how you do it, just do it. Make sure no one ever finds her. I don't want this coming back to bite us in the ass."

"What if someone comes looking for her?"

"Like who James? Her parents who haven't called her in years because they don't give a fuck about her? People from a job she doesn't have? Seriously, use your brain."

"There is one person who's going to be a problem."

"And who is that, James?"

"Anthony. He won't let something like this happen to Cindy."

"Then get rid of him, too. Like I said already, I will not wait around forever."

"Okay, I will do it. Just give me a little time to plan something out. If I do this, then it needs to be done right. The last thing I need is to be sitting in prison over her worthless life."

"Good boy, James. I love you. Please don't forget that we don't have much time left before the 'you know what' happens. You need to hurry before it's too late."

"I know this. It crosses my mind every single day. Love you too. I have to get back to the office. I will see you on my next work trip," he said.

"They both laughed, gave each other a kiss, and walked out. I waited about fifteen minutes after they left to leave. I mean, what the hell, Cindy? Can you believe this? They want to kill us so they can be together. What are we going to do about it? We can't go to the police because Ethan will just run to James and then do nothing about it."

"Anthony, relax. I will make sure that piece of shit gets what is coming to him. He's going to get exactly what he deserves."

Then it hit me. "Oh my gosh, Dr. Lisa, I just realized you can't let James come back here to see me or he will try to kill me."

"Okay Cindy, let's not get ahead of ourselves. How about we talk more about this tomorrow?"

"Okay," I said.

After a few hours, Vicky came in to see me. She was such a welcome sight after lying around bored out of my head. If I'm not crazy already, this place is definitely going to make me crazy.

"Hey girlfriend, how are you doing? Are you feeling any better?"

"I'm better now that you're here, Vicky. This place is driving me insane. You look great and you smell good. I've smelled that perfume before, I just can't remember where. It smells great. How are you?"

"I'm good. I just got everything finalized for my next club opening. How are they treating you here?"

"Okay, I guess. I have to talk to a shrink everyday thanks to James. I could strangle him for running his mouth to the doctor."

She sat down on the edge of my bed and placed her hand on my knee. "He's just worried about you, sweetie. We both are. We just want you to get better so you can get out of here and get back home."

"Well, I know why James wants me out of here. He wants to kill me and Anthony. I was talking to Dr. Lisa about it today."

"Who's Dr. Lisa?"

"She's my psychiatrist."

Vicky grabbed me by the hand. "Listen Cindy, you know I love you and I would never lie to you. There is no Anthony, sweetie. I don't know why you continue to believe this?"

"Vicky, please believe me. James hired him. He stays at the house to work the farm for me."

She let out a sigh. "Honey, I've seen no one at the house. I even asked James, and he doesn't know who Anthony is. And believe me, I would have seen him by now. I've been staying there on the weekends, so I don't have to keep traveling back and forth like I do all week. It's been quite the task to take care of the animals and the house. Now I know how you felt and I'm not doing as much as you did around there. But, yes, there is no guy named Anthony there."

"Maybe James fired him after I got hurt and he is lying to you. Anthony stopped by to visit me. I saw him in the hall. He looked over at me and said 'I love you' through the window."

Vicky perked up. "He didn't come in to see you? Why would he come here and not come in to visit with you?"

"He got frightened by something and ran off before he could. Right after he took off, James came into my room. He might have left because he saw James and he knows James wants to kill the both of us. I already told you this, Vicky."

"That sounds so silly, Cindy. I can't ever imagine James hurting you, or killing you. Why would you think he would do something like that?"

"I know it's true because Anthony told me."

"Cindy, sweetie, you want me to believe James wants you dead because a man, only you know and only you can see, told you so?"

"Vicky, please, you need to believe me. I'm not crazy. I might not remember how I got here, but I remember everything leading up to my accident."

"Cindy, even if this was all true, which I don't believe it is, what reason would James have to want you dead?"

"Anthony overheard him talking to another woman at a coffee shop. James has been having an affair all throughout our marriage and they want Anthony and I out of the picture."

"What? Did he say who this woman was?"

"He didn't know. He had never seen her before."

"So let me get this straight, Cindy. A guy nobody has ever seen told you your husband was with a woman he had never seen, and they want to kill you and this unknown guy Anthony because your husband is having an affair? Did I get all that right?"

"Yes, Vicky!"

"Cindy, do you see why I am having a hard time believing all of this?"

"Listen, I know it seems crazy, but I'm telling you the truth. You need to believe me. Don't act like them and treat me like I'm crazy. Please, Vicky."

"I don't think you're crazy, Cindy. I think you suffered a serious brain injury and you need some help to distinguish between what is real and what is only in your head. You need to get help and get better. It's going to take some time. Someday you will look back at this and laugh about it."

"What did you just say to me? You think I'm crazy and imagining things? I thought you were my friend. This isn't a joke. You know what, Vicky? I don't need you either. To hell with all of you. The only person who I can count on and will ever need is Anthony. Get out of my room and don't come back."

"Cindy, please don't do this."

"Get out, Vicky! Now!"

She grabbed a tissue from the box and began to pat her eyes with it. Then she walked out of my room. It hurt me to see her go, but I couldn't believe she would treat me like this. She is my best friend and I could always count on her to take my side, no matter what the situation was. Why is she acting this way? She always stood up for me and protected me and now she is turning on me? Why is everyone acting this way? I can't take much more of this. I'm seriously going to snap.

I imagined Anthony running into my room and picking me up out of my bed, holding me and telling me he's here to rescue me. I want him to carry me out of this room and take me away. I think about leaving with him and going far, far away where we can be together forever, just him and I. As soon as I get out of here, that's what I'm going to do, I'm going to find him and we are going to spend the rest of our lives together, until the day we die. He is all that matters to me.

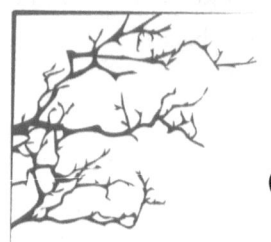

Chapter 13

I spent the better part of an hour sitting on the edge of my bed and staring out the window at the mountains in the distance. I don't know how long I will last being cooped up in this hospital, and I wish I knew how long I am going to be here for. I wonder what Anthony is doing? I can only hope I'm on his mind as much as he is on mine. My heart aches for him so much.

I can't seem to shake this feeling of loneliness. It's giving me anxiety. Anthony is the only person I have left, and he's not here with me. I have the same feeling deep down in my stomach I used to get all the time growing up. It's a scary feeling to be alone. Yes, this hospital is bustling with staff and patients, but not having someone I know personally to interact with is depressing. I wish I could pick up the phone and have one person I could call, but I have no one. This solitude is smothering me like a wet blanket and seems to follow me wherever I go.

Anthony is the only person in my life who cares for me. There has been nobody else I could truly count on. Something as simple as human interaction is often overlooked by those who have people in their lives. Until you have been here, you could never understand how being alone can suck the life right out of you. It's terrifying, actually.

This loneliness seems to follow me through life. The only time I never felt alone is with Anthony. There was a short time after I met James that I didn't feel alone, but I was never at peace like I was with Anthony. There has always been an uneasy feeling I have with James. There is something deep down inside that makes me feel like I can't trust him, and I have always felt that way about him. I never should have married him. I thought I was in love, but I now realize it wasn't true love.

I guess I gravitated to James for the attention he gave me early in our relationship. After growing up with my parents, I took any attention I could get from people. Thinking back to when I met James, I didn't know what love was, either. My parents never showed me what love is like. Meeting James made me feel different at the time and different was better than what I have always felt.

If there were a way I could go back in time, I would have waited for the love I deserve. The kind of love everybody deserves. I think about my parents from time to time and it only causes me hurt and frustration. How can two people not have an emotional attachment to a person who comes from them? How could they look their daughter in the face and not feel something for her? I don't know how the two people who created her can overlook and forget an innocent child. Are people really heartless mostly, and I just don't know any better? If there is one thing I can count on with my parents, it's that I will never hear from them again. I really hate them with everything I have. Sometimes I wish they would call me only so I can ask them one question: why did you not love me?

Until I met Anthony, I would go through stages of self hate. I would ask myself why no one loved me enough to want to spend time with me. There has always been this feeling toward myself like I wasn't good enough for anyone. It must be my fault why no one loves me, I always thought.

Anthony changed a lot of those feelings I had about myself. It's almost as if he freed me from a life of imprisonment. I felt trapped in a cage of despair my whole life until I met him. As much as I love him, I am feeling alone again without him here. My soul hurts and it feels torn apart, if that's possible. I can't go on without him much longer. He is the only thing that keeps me going every day. If I lose Anthony, I will no longer have a reason to live. He is all I have.

I laid back down on my bed. There is nothing else to do. I no longer have an appetite and can barely eat. The only thing that helps pass the time is sleep. I wish I could stay asleep until the day I get out of here. It's too depressing to be stuck here.

Dr. Lisa prescribed me some medications, but I don't trust her or the drugs, so I pretend to swallow them and then I flush them down the toilet. Knowing her, I'm sure they are antipsychotic pills. I'm not crazy, so I won't medicate myself with harmful drugs.

I closed my eyes, hoping to fall back asleep so I can wake up one more day closer to my release. My brain blocked everything out, and I felt at peace. It felt like I was dreaming. There are footsteps in my room and I can't tell if they are real or not. I'm so close to falling asleep, I don't want to open my eyes. I waited for them to stop, but they kept going. Is there someone here?

I pushed myself to wake up and open my eyes. There, at the end of my bed, was James, pacing back and forth. He seemed confused and bothered by something.

"James, what are you doing here?"

He stopped pacing and turned to look at me, then he placed his hand on his chin and started tapping his cheek with his finger.

"Cindy, Cindy, Cindy," he said, while piercing my eyes with his.

"Yes, James?"

"Cindy, I'm trying to figure out what I'm going to do about you."

"I'm so sorry, James. I don't quite follow what you're saying. What do you mean?"

He went over to the chair next to my bed and sat down, still staring at me. I started to get uncomfortable with him being here. "James, you should probably go. I'm not feeling well today."

He just sat there looking at me and ignoring my request for him to leave. His head tilted to the side as he looked at me with curiosity. It seemed like he didn't know what to say to me and then he spoke. "I'm puzzled, Cindy. After everything I have done for you, I thought you would appreciate me more than you do. As a matter of fact, I don't think you appreciate me at all."

"James, what are you talking about?"

He lifted his finger and placed it on his mouth, signaling me to stop talking. "Shh, Cindy. Stop talking. I didn't come here to listen to you talk." He started stroking his chin and whispered to himself, "What am I to do about you?" Then he said, "Cindy, let me see if I have this right. First, you were a nobody, and no one wanted anything to do with you. Even your own parents wanted nothing to do with you. I should have thought about that one a little more and seen the red flags. I mean, how much of a loser do you have to be in order for your own mom and dad to not love you? But, me being the nice guy I am, didn't see it at the time. Not only did I not see it, I rescued poor little Cindy from her delusional fucked up life. I should have let you rot in your parents' house. Instead, I give you a home of your own and a better life that you don't deserve. Marrying you is the biggest mistake I have ever made, but I did that as well. I go to work everyday just to give you a good life and you know what I get?"

I started to cry. Why is he doing this to me? Is it not enough to be in here after having the back of my head crushed in?

"Stop crying, poor Cindy. Hey look everybody, I'm crying and need a pity party. You're a joke. I thought I was helping you by giving you a life of your own, but as usual, Cindy only cares about herself. You couldn't keep your messed up life to yourself. You had to let your dysfunctional behavior screw up my life, too."

Tears kept rolling down my cheeks, no matter how hard I tried to contain them. Is this what my life has become? How long must I tolerate this abuse before I have to end it all?

James got up from the chair with his gaze still fixed on me. "I think it's time I finally take care of you for good?"

"Take care of me? What do you mean?"

He walked over to the hall window and closed the curtain. "I'm sorry, Cindy, but we can't go on like this anymore." Then he stood at the side of my bed and placed his hand on my forehead.

"Please go James, I'm begging you. I will do whatever you want. Just go, you're making me nervous. Please."

He pushed down on my head. The pain I felt made me cringe. "Ow, James, let go of me. Stop it."

"Shh, Cindy. This will all be over before you know it." Then he placed his other hand over my mouth and nose and began to suffocate me. I struggled, trying to get him off of me. I tried to pull his hand away, but he was too strong. I thrashed around on the bed as panic took over me. Just when I thought I was going to pass out, the monitor next to my bed started beeping really loud and fast, saving my life.

James got frightened and pulled away from me just in time before a nurse came running in. As I was trying to catch my breath, I heard him say to the nurse, "Oh good, you're here. I was ready to go get someone. I was sitting in the chair waiting for her to wake up and she just started freaking out. I'm not sure what is wrong with her. I think she is having a panic attack. She seems to be having another episode again."

The nurse rushed over to my bed. "Cindy, are you okay? Calm down and take a deep breath."

"He tried to kill me. He put his hand on my face and tried to suffocate me."

"Okay, calm down. I will get you something to help you relax."

"No, don't leave me in here with him. He's trying to kill me."

James walked over to my bedside and touched my hand. "Cindy, it's okay. You were just having another hallucination. I love you. Just calm down."

I pulled my hand away from him. "Get your hand off of me! Don't you ever touch me again! You will not get away with this. Leave now, James."

The nurse turned toward James and asked him to leave so I could calm down. He walked out the door, only stopping momentarily to look back at me and smile.

The nurse came back and gave me a sedative to calm me down. "Please don't let him back in here with me. I'm begging you."

"I won't let him back in here, I promise. I will make sure nobody comes in here without your approval from now on if it makes you feel better." Then she opened the curtain and went back to her desk.

I don't know what is happening to me. I'm beginning to question my own sanity. Everybody seems to think I'm having hallucinations. I know I suffered a terrible head injury, but I can't be this messed up. I wish I knew the truth. I feel like I'm living in a nightmare I can't wake up from. I need Anthony. He will know what is happening to me and tell me the truth. He is the only one I can trust at this point.

It wasn't long before the medication put me to sleep.

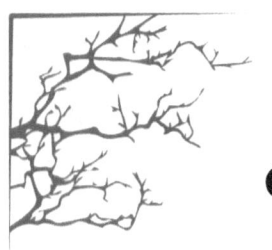

Chapter 14

"Cindy, wake up. It's time for our daily session," Dr. Lisa said.

"I'm up, gosh, do you ever take a day off? It's kind of annoying," I said.

"Okay, take a minute to wake up while I settle into the chair and get my notes in order. How are you feeling today?"

"Well, let's see. I feel depressed, hurt, alone, betrayed, and trapped. Oh, and let's not forget, annoyed by your presence."

"Why do you feel like this?"

"I got a visit from Vicky. I told her about James's affair and how he wanted to kill me and Anthony. She told me I was crazy, and she didn't believe me."

"Cindy, it must be hard when people you care about don't believe you?"

"Yeah, I mean, she's supposed to be my best friend, and she doesn't even believe Anthony exists after I told her he does."

"Did you talk to her about why she feels this way?"

"No, I kicked her out of my room. I told her to leave and to never come back."

"You said she is your best friend, so I'm assuming that the two of you are close. You met in college, right?"

"Yes, we are close. We talk about everything."

"Do you value your relationship with Vicky?"

"Yes, I do, but not as much as I value my relationship with Anthony. I would get rid of anyone in my life for him."

"Tell me, Cindy, what is Anthony to you? How much do you value him and what does your relationship with him mean to you?"

"My relationship with Anthony means everything to me. I can't imagine my life without him. There is nothing I wouldn't do for him or us. If I couldn't have him in my life, then I wouldn't want to live. I love him and need him so much that I... I would kill for him."

"What about yourself, Cindy? Do you value yourself?"

"I guess. I don't know what you mean?"

"Okay, you just said you would kill for Anthony. Let's hope you would never commit such an act of violence against anyone causing them to lose their life. Now, let's just say, if you had the choice of walking away from an incident to protect yourself or spend the rest of your life in prison to protect Anthony, what would you choose to do?"

"That's so easy. Obviously, I would choose prison if it meant protecting the love of my life."

"So you would put his needs above your own?"

"Yes."

"So, would you say you value Anthony's life over your own? Do you value your life at all?"

"Of course I value my life. I'm what makes Anthony happy, and without me, he wouldn't be happy."

"So, Cindy, what you are telling me, just to be clear, is the only value you find in yourself, is your ability to make Anthony happy?"

"Yes, I mean, no. I guess I like the fact I can make James miserable too, and I enjoy being responsible for his suffering after finding out the truth about him."

Dr. Lisa glanced up at me. "And is that all? Are those two things the only things that keep you going every day?"

"Yup, that pretty much sums it up. I wasn't lying when I told you I couldn't live without Anthony."

"I know, Cindy. I believe you feel that way. What about James? How do you feel about your husband? Do you find any value in him?"

"Are you referring to the piece of shit I married? Because if you are, then you will hear nothing nice about him coming out of my mouth. Write this down in your notes...Cindy hates James with a passion and wishes he would save us all the trouble and die!"

"Do you really believe James is trying to kill you and Anthony?"

"Yes, I do."

"How does that make you feel?"

"At first I was a little scared for Anthony's sake, but when I found out James has been having an affair all along and now wants to kill me, it pisses me off real bad. So, why would I have any value for someone who has done nothing but hurt me and who now wants to kill me and my soulmate? I wish I would have gone through with it when I had the chance."

"Wish you would have gone through with what?"

"Killing James."

"You were going to kill your husband?"

"Yeah, I got real close to doing it, too. I wanted to protect my sweet, precious Anthony. There is no way I was going to let James hurt my love. I stood over him one night while he slept, holding a knife, trying to convince myself to kill him. He moved his arm, and it caused me to panic and run back out of the room."

"Cindy, what you just admitted to me is very serious and concerning. I don't know how we move forward with this information. Do you feel you are a danger to other people, especially your husband?"

"No, if I were a danger to anyone, especially James, then he would be dead already. I didn't go through with it. If you knew how he started treating me and how he abused me, you would understand. I will admit, I didn't help the situation by doing things to get under his skin, but the way I saw it was, if I didn't have it in me to kill him, then I was at least going to live my life how I wanted to and also do whatever I could to make him miserable. Even if it made him more angry. Little did I know at the time how abusive toward me he was going to get."

"I remember one day when I wanted to get under his skin."

It was a Saturday, I think, and I slept most of the morning away. James was home for the weekend. He was leaving the coming Friday to fly out to "who gives a fuck where!" I was hoping his plane would crash and save me the trouble of having to kill him myself. I heard him typing away in his office. Ugh, I hate him. I've never been this mad at anybody in my entire life. Even the girl who bullied me in school would get a free pass on life if it came down to her or James. I wanted revenge on him in the worst way. I wanted to make him pay. I didn't have the courage to kill him, so I was going to get back at him another way.

One morning, after waking up on the couch, I sat up and looked at my clothes that were in a pile on the floor. Let's see how much he likes this, I thought. I stood up, naked, folded my blanket and walked down the hall toward his office room. His door was wide open. I stopped and stood in his doorway. He looked up at me and said, "Do you plan on wearing some clothes today?"

"Maybe, I haven't decided yet. Have you seen Anthony?"

"No, why?" he asked.

"No reason, James. If you see him, make sure you tell him I'm looking for him and I need him real bad. I need him to do something for me. Like, bad." I decided to lie to James and say, "I went looking out back for him, but I couldn't find him."

James's face got red. He snapped at me with an angry tone. "You were walking around outside looking for him like that?"

"Yes, I was. It's such a shame I didn't find him. Oops, I forgot to put my clothes in the washer. I better go do that now." I turned and walked to the laundry room at the other end of the house, grabbing my clothes from the floor along the way.

I could sense his blood pressure rising. I never walked around the house naked when it was just him and I. I put my clothes in the washer and started heading to the bedroom to grab a dress. As I was walking through the kitchen area, I heard a buzzing noise. It was James's phone on the counter. I went over and glanced at it. It was a text message from Vicky. It read: Hey, are you on one of your "work trips" ??? Call me. Why is she texting James and why did she say "work trips" like that? It seemed strange. I picked up the phone and brought it down to him. "Here, your phone made a buzzing noise."

He asked, "Who is it?"

"I don't know. I didn't check. Oh, also, I decided I am going to wear some clothes today... you know... only because you're here and just like you don't want your psycho wife lying next to you, I don't want my pervert husband looking at my body. I decided I will keep the clothes off only when you're not around." Then I walked out and went to the bedroom. I knew I was playing with fire and I was enjoying every second.

I stood in the closet, going through my light summer dresses. I already knew what I was going to do to get back at James. Although he would not know, it will make me feel much better inside. And yes, it involves Anthony.

I was looking through my clothes to find the shortest, skimpiest dress I could find. I found the perfect one, and it is the shortest dress I own. It sits above the midpoint of my thighs, and it's short enough that you can see everything from behind if I lean over. It is a thin, light white material with a cute red floral pattern. I must wear white undies and a white bra to blend in with it, or you can see right through it when it's pressed up against my skin. And today, there will be no bra or undies included in this outfit.

As far as not having sex with Anthony when James is home, that changes today. I will not make it obvious, out of fear of what James might do to Anthony, but I am going to do it just so I feel like I'm handing out some form of retribution.

I took a shower, brushed my teeth and hair, slipped into my dress and put my pink cowgirl boots on. I was feeling promiscuous and wanted to be a dirty girl, so I went in search of Anthony. I soon found him in the barn, standing by the horses. As I went over to him, I grabbed his hand and walked him upstairs to the hayloft. I opened the door at the front of the barn so I could see the backside of the house in case James came walking outside. I stood with my back to the wall next to the door.

Anthony asked, "What are we doing up here?"

"That piece of shit I'm married to pisses me off."

He looked at me, unsure of what was going on. "And?" he asked.

"And you're going to stand here and have sex with his wife right up against this wall."

He stared out the door and down at the house. "If he catches us, he will kill us, Cindy."

I pulled my dress off, threw it on top of the hay, and stood there wearing nothing but my boots. "Don't watch the house. You keep your eyes on me," I ordered him.

"But what if he comes out, Cindy?"

"Listen to me! Be a man and get over here! Unless you want to go back to doing whatever it was you were doing before I came out?"

"No, I want to be right here," he said, staring at my naked body.

I leaned my shoulders back into the wall, inviting him to take me. He stepped forward and gave me exactly what I came for. It was thrilling and exciting taking that kind of risk while James was sitting in the house, close by.

"Thank you, handsome. I really needed that."

I put my dress back on. Anthony went back to what he was doing, and I went into the house to get my chores done. As I was walking past James's office, on my way to get his dirty laundry for the wash, he asked, in a smart condescending way, "Were you able to find Anthony?"

I stopped and looked through the doorway, smiling from ear to ear. "Yes, I did as a matter of fact and he did exactly, and I mean exactly, what I needed him to do," I said.

The angry tone in his voice said it all. "Yeah, that's good," he said.

I walked away, saying under my breath, "No, it was great asshole".

I spent the rest of the day picking up around the house and cooking. Mashed potatoes, barbecued chicken breast and corn on the cob were on the menu tonight. I'm not the best cook, but it came out pretty good. I guess being forced to cook for myself at such a young age paid off.

Time seemed to fly by. It's crazy how fast the day goes by when you're excited and have such an amazing guy like Anthony on your mind. After our little "Get together", he took a shower and sat in the living room to watch television. I think he was there to watch me while I cleaned up the kitchen. Every time I looked over at him, I would catch him staring at me and giving me a smile. I would smile back. It kept me in a great mood. I also didn't have James's stupid face to look at either. He spent the day in his office watching television, working or doing whatever the hell it is he does to avoid me. It's better that way, for the both of us, and it made me feel good inside to get back at James in my own way.

After I did the dishes, I spent the rest of the night next to Anthony on the couch watching television. Any time that James would go to the kitchen for something, I would look at Anthony and giggle or smile while I put my hand on his leg just to get under James's skin even more.

Dr. Lisa stopped me. "Okay, Cindy, we are going to end it for the day. After the things that you told me today, there will be a couple of things done differently while you are here. I'm going to put you at a higher risk level, so the staff will monitor you more frequently and you're only going to have supervised visitation from here on out for your husband's safety. Do you understand what I am saying to you?"

"Fine, it doesn't bother me one bit. I doubt James or Vicky will come back, and I can only hope Anthony comes to see me again. As far as Anthony, I think it's safe to say I wouldn't harm a single hair on his head."

"Alright then, tomorrow we will meet again. Promise me you will be on your best behavior."

"I promise," I said.

I wasted the day away taking naps. It's not a big deal for me. If I sleep too much throughout the day and can't sleep at night, I tell the nurse I'm having a hard time sleeping and she gives me something to help.

I thought about my visit with James yesterday. I'm still shaken by it. The more I think about it, the more I convince myself he tried to suffocate me. My head still hurts from him pushing on it. I also have a small cut on the inside of my lip from him placing his hand over my mouth. If I were hallucinating, then how did I get a cut?

Sometimes when I look through the hall window, I can see James standing there, looking at me with a grin on his face. I have to close my eyes and tell myself he's not really there, then he goes away.

Night time is the worst for me here. I know there are still plenty of staff working, but the atmosphere is different. The hospital is a darker place at night and there's not much going on. Everyone is quiet and not moving around like they do during the day.

Waking up is becoming difficult for me. It terrifies me. I seem to be okay when someone wakes me and I know who it is. If I wake up on my own, I lay here with my eyes closed for a few minutes, afraid to open them. I don't know what to expect when my eyes open. I lay here listening for anyone that might be inside of my room. My biggest fear now is seeing James standing over me when I wake up. As soon as I'm convinced no one is here, I slowly open them just to make sure.

I wish I knew how long they plan on keeping me for? At what point is it safe for me to leave? Do they know when a brain heals completely? Sometimes I think about getting up and walking out. They can't keep me here if I don't want to be here. I think the only reason I am staying is because I don't want to go home to James. There really isn't anywhere else I can go. If he is willing to try to kill me inside of a hospital, what would he do to me as soon as I walked into our house?

I wish there was a way I could get hold of Anthony. He would know what to do. I wonder where he is staying and if he is okay? I better not find out James did something to him or I will go off the deep end. I hope I see Anthony again soon. It's becoming too much of a struggle for me to make it through each day.

Maybe James is right and I'm the reason no one has loved me until Anthony came along. Does Anthony not see what everyone else in my life sees? Am I so messed up that I ruin the lives of those around me? It's depressing to think my life might be worthless. I can't think about it. The day is passing by and nightfall is creeping in. I need to clear my head.

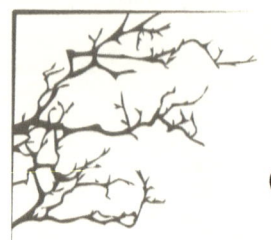

Chapter 15

I was feeling restless. I needed to get out of this room. Being stuck in here is enough to drive someone out of their mind. I paged the nurse, hoping she could get me out of here, even if it's only for a few minutes. Once she came in, I pleaded with her. "Can you please take me out of this room? I'm going stir crazy. I need a change of scenery. Please?" I begged her.

"I don't see why not. Let me finish my rounds and I will get one of the other nurses to help me get you into a chair. You might not weigh that much, but I'm not strong enough to catch you if you fall."

About forty minutes later, she came back into my room, pushing a wheelchair with another nurse. They helped me get into the chair. It was somewhat of a struggle at first to keep my balance since I've spent all this time lying in bed. Or it could just be the drugs. I have leg exercises I do everyday per the doctor's request to strengthen myself even though I don't feel like I need it.

"So, Miss Cindy, how do you feel about going outside and getting some fresh air for a little while? It's a warm, beautiful night out."

"I would love that so much," I said.

She wheeled me down a couple of halls, into the elevator, then down a few more halls with turns. Once she pushed me through the exit doors, I could feel the beautiful, fresh night air engulf me. It felt so good. It even smelled amazing and made me miss my farm. The smell of the night air and grass reminded me of my life at home. I tipped my head back and closed my eyes to imagine the rolling fields around my house.

As soon as I felt the chair stop, I opened my eyes. Wow! It's so pretty. I forgot how beautiful the night sky is. It looks like a big dark canvas, glittering with millions of bright stars. The sky is full of them. It made me think of the night Anthony and I went camping and how I stared up at the same stars while he made love to me.

Anthony asked me, out of nowhere one day, "Hey baby, what would you think about going camping with me some night soon?"

"You mean like outside and on the ground? I'm not so sure, but I guess we can try it. No promises I will like it, though. If I don't, can we pack up and come back?"

"Of course we can come back anytime you decide you want to leave. You make it sound so horrible by saying outside and on the ground."

He grabbed me, pulled me close to him, and put his arms around me. "I just want you to know, when I say camping, I mean on horses, you and I laying next to a fire, underneath a blanket and the stars, making love. Then me holding you tight all night long to keep you warm. Also, did I mention I will be the one cooking you dinner for once and then breakfast in the morning, over the fire?"

"What? If you're going to put it like that, then I'm in. Sign me up. We are going camping."

"Outstanding, Cindy. So, when do you want to go?"

"Well, you make it sound so good. How about tomorrow night?"

"You know your husband will be home, right?"

"We will see about that. I think I have a plan. I will be your Bonnie and you can be my Clyde. First, we will get some good sleep tonight, and then in the morning we will go to town and get groceries for our trip."

"I'm not sure I like the sound of that, Cindy. The Bonnie and Clyde thing? What do you have up your sleeve, my hot criminal?"

"You're just going to wait and find out, I guess."

That night, we went to bed early so we could get to the supermarket when it opened. I was so excited to go camping, which isn't like me. Don't get me wrong, I love to get my hands dirty working on a farm, but sleeping on the ground was never my thing. But sleeping on the ground next to Anthony is a totally different story altogether.

After James left in the morning, we got ready to go, giving James a head start before we left. We drove into town and stopped at the store. Anthony ran in while I waited in the truck. It wasn't long before he came out with the groceries, smiling.

"What are you smiling at, troublemaker?"

"Your beautiful face through the windshield. This is going to be fun," he said.

I asked him, "Are you ready to execute my plan?"

He looked at me with a playful smile. "It seems I don't have a choice. We are in too deep now that I bought us steaks for dinner."

I drove across town to James's office.

"Cindy, isn't this where James works?"

"Yup."

"And we are here... why?"

"You'll see."

I pulled down the street and parked out of sight.

"Come on Anthony, let's go. Keep an eye out for James's car."

We made our way to the parking lot and found his car sitting in between two other cars.

"Here, take this while I keep a lookout," I said. I reached into my pocket, pulled out a knife, and handed it to him.

"Cindy, what do you want me to do with this?"

"Flatten his tires, Anthony. Hurry while no one is coming."

I kept watching and then heard a hissing noise coming from the first tire he had punctured. It didn't take long before they were all losing air.

"Okay, Cindy, I'm done. Let's get the hell out of here before someone spots us." We scurried away, back to the truck, jumping in as fast as we could.

"Wow, what a rush. Cindy, that was crazy. We make a great team."

"I know. Wait until we do the bank job I have lined up for us."

"What!" he screeched.

I started laughing so hard at his response. "I'm kidding, Anthony. I'm just kidding."

"Girl, you're going to get it, and that's a promise."

"Sounds hot. Don't make promises you can't keep," I said.

Anthony placed his hand on my leg. "So, now what do we do, baby?"

"We go home, finish getting ready, and wait for a phone call. If I know James like I think I do, he will not want to deal with his car after he finds it like that. My guess is he will call a tow truck to bring his car to a garage so it can get fixed while he spends the night at a nearby hotel. That way, he makes it back to work in the morning."

"And if he doesn't do that?"

"Then we figure something else out. Either way, no matter what happens, you're still cooking for me tonight. You aren't getting out of that, no matter how hard you try."

"For you, Cindy, anything."

We went home and continued to get things ready. Anthony saddled up the horses and packed what he could on them. The rest of the stuff we put into backpacks. It wasn't long before James called me with the bad news about his car. He wasn't coming home tonight. He won't be home until tomorrow night after he gets his car from the shop. Mission accomplished.

We finished packing up the horses and headed out on our little adventure. "So, where is my knight in shining armor taking me?"

"Just a few hills that way. I figured it would be close enough to home in case you want to go back and the horses can graze without being able to leave the property. I also want to let you know the pile of firewood I already have there has nothing to do with us staying where we are going," he said.

"Oh, it doesn't? Why don't I believe you?"

"Okay, I might be telling a little white lie. I chopped and split some wood a few weeks ago because I wanted to get out here and spend a night under the stars. It's piled up under the big willow tree out in the field. I figured it's the perfect spot to spend the night. I've been waiting for the right time to get you out here with me."

It didn't take long before we got to the place Anthony had picked out. We unpacked and unsaddled the horses so they could graze out in the field. I laid a few heavy blankets down and unpacked while Anthony made a fire pit and started a fire.

"Anthony, it's so beautiful out here. The smell of fresh grass and wildflowers is so refreshing and the warm sun just feels amazing on my skin. I don't think I would ever want to live anywhere else. And having you to share it with makes me feel complete. We don't need to discuss it now and ruin our time together, but at some point, I want to talk about our future. I can't imagine ever having to live one minute of my life without you. I love you so much. Promise me you will never leave me."

"I promise I will never, ever, leave you. You mean the world to me and I also can't imagine living my life without you. Cindy, I love you more than you could ever imagine."

I looked at Anthony with a smile. "The sun is going to be down soon. Do you plan on feeding the love of your life?"

"Yes, I'm getting ready to cook dinner once the fire dies down a little."

"You didn't bring a pan. How do you plan on cooking this amazing dinner you planned for me?"

"Watch and learn," he said.

It's amazing how crafty Anthony is. He cut up potatoes, wrapped them in aluminum foil with butter, and tossed them on the hot coals to cook. He also did the same with the corn on the cob. I was curious about how he was going to cook the steak until I watched him put sticks into the ground and hang the steaks over the fire. This man is amazing. Once dinner was done, he put it on a plate and said, "Here you go, one delicious meal, cooked over a fire, in the great outdoors."

We sat on the blankets and ate. Dinner was delicious, as promised. I enjoyed sitting with Anthony, alone together, and admiring our surroundings. "Thank you so much, Anthony. It was so delicious. How did you learn to cook like that or do any of the amazing things you do? You are so good with your hands."

"I learned a lot from my dad when I was growing up. He was a tough cowboy who liked to live off of the land. He did ranch work, farming, taught me how to fix a lot of things and took me camping a lot. My carpentry skills, I learned from the first job I ever got."

"Are your parents still together?"

"No, my dad passed away from lung cancer when I was a young teen and my mom died about 12 years later. She was a tough woman. She raised my brother and I by herself until she passed. Once she died, my brother and I went to stay with our uncle after the farm went into foreclosure. At some point, we both went our separate ways until I started coming down here to stay with him for work."

"I'm sorry about your parents."

"Don't be. It's all part of life."

"Anthony, look at all the fireflies. They are so beautiful."

"I agree. Lay with me so we can gaze at the stars together," he said.

He laid down, and I snuggled right up to him. The stars were so pretty to look at.

"Speaking of life, Anthony, would you ever consider having a child?"

"I never thought about it, Cindy. If you and I, at some point, got married, I would consider it. I would start a family with you if that's something you also wanted."

"Oh my gosh, Anthony. You know what to say to make a girl's head spin. I feel like I'm going to melt away. Are you saying that you will marry me?"

"Cindy, yes, I want to marry you."

"Oh my gosh, Anthony! I want to marry you too. Let's get married."

"So is that yes, Cindy? Will you marry me?"

"Yes, baby, I will marry you over and over. I love you so much."

"Before I do, wife to be, I need to make love to you, right here, under the stars."

I smiled at him and said, "I wouldn't want it any other way."

I woke up, just as the sun was coming up, after one of the best nights of my life. It wasn't just how Anthony made passionate love to me; it was also because he asked me to marry him and said he wanted to start a family together. I have never been so happy in my entire life as I was right now. I want to get rid of James right away and start my life with Anthony as soon as possible.

I rolled over, and that beautiful man of mine was already cooking breakfast for me. We ate and then packed up the horses for our quick trip home. Once we started riding off, I stopped and turned my horse around to get one last good look at where we spent our special night together and where Anthony proposed to me. Anthony stopped and turned around as well.

"Look how beautiful that willow tree is, Anthony. That tree is always going to have a special place in my heart now. Willow, that's perfect. If we ever have a daughter, I want to name her Willow, so I will forever remember our night together under that tree."

"That sounds perfect, Cindy. Willow is such a pretty name. So I take it you enjoyed your night on the ground with me?"

"Oh, did I ever. It was fantastic, and I loved it. Thank you so much for doing this with me. I needed this."

"No problem. We should do this again sometime," he said.

It felt so good to think about that night with Anthony. The nurse brought me back into my room and I thanked her for doing what she did for me. For the first time since I woke up in this hospital, I laid in bed, happy and smiling. Thinking about my special night with Anthony gave me something greater to look forward to. I didn't care that I was here, and I didn't care about James, Vicky, or the doctors. I had no worries, and it was so freeing, knowing it wouldn't be long before I was with the man of my dreams again. I slept like a baby.

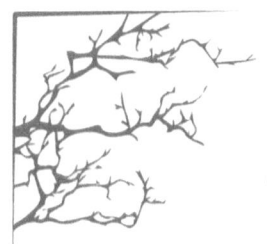

Chapter 16

"Good morning, Cindy. How was your night? Did you rest well?"

"Yes, Dr. Lisa. I had a wonderful night. I was in a good mood for the first time since being here. The nurse took me outside for a little while and it did wonders for my well-being. It's funny how many little things in life we take for granted, like the stars and the fresh air. I hope I get to go out and do it again soon."

"Cindy, that's wonderful. My husband and I still sit out on our porch on warm nights, looking up at the night sky and talking. It's soothing for the soul."

"Yeah, I agree. I never paid much attention to the stars before, but now I find them very romantic. Anthony gave me a new appreciation for them. Now, when I look up at the stars, I think of him and everything he has done for me. He has changed me because I never thought I could love someone the way I love him, yet I do. When he came into my life, I was at rock bottom. I'm not sure how much longer I would have lasted. I thought, this is all my life is ever going to be, misery and pain, and I already lived that way growing up. I thought marrying James would be my way out of the hell I was living in, but I was so wrong. Never for a minute did I think he would throw me right back into hopelessness and depression. Anthony was my guiding angel, who rescued me from the pit of despair. I owe him everything. I can't wait to get back to him."

"Cindy, I know how much Anthony means to you right now, but have you ever thought about how you would handle him letting you down? No one is perfect. We all have our flaws and sometimes people let you down. How do you think you would handle it?"

"I'm sure I will be fine. I don't think I could ever be mad at him for long. There is something about him that differs from other people. Also, he loves me, like really loves me. I can ask him for anything and he would do it. James doesn't love me. He knows what hurts me and continues on doing those things. How can you say you love someone and continue to keep hurting them? Anthony treats me like I'm his queen, like he never wants to lose me. He appreciates everything about me and shows it by the way he treats me. I'm so lucky to have him. I don't know where I would be right now if Anthony never walked into my life."

"Cindy, would you say that you love Anthony or would you say you have an obsession with him?"

"I think it's both. I love him more than life and I am very obsessed with him also, but I think it's a healthy obsession. It's no different from the guy who is a huge baseball fan and has to get his fix by watching the games and supporting his team. So yeah, I guess you can say that I'm a huge fan of Anthony and his love for me."

"Cindy, sometimes an obsession can become very unhealthy, especially for the person on the receiving end. It can make people feel uneasy and make them feel like they have no personal space. In extreme cases, some people make irrational decisions such as stalking, threatening or even harming the person who they believe they love for the sake of their own satisfaction."

"That's not the case with Anthony and I. He seems to have the same obsession towards me and it just works for the two of us. We both hate when we're apart, but we also understand sometimes we have to be. That's just life."

"Okay, Cindy, I just want to let you know that my entire morning is free today, so if it seems like we are talking for too long, just let me know and we can get back to it another time. I don't want you to feel like you're being pushed to continue on."

"Okay," I said.

"So tell me, Cindy, I want to know what life will be like for you, moving forward. How do you picture your future? Give me a glimpse into what you think the future holds for you."

"It's a life I could never have with James. I want children and I could never have kids with my husband. I would end up raising our children all by myself and have to watch them grow up, hating their dad, for never being around."

"I see myself married to Anthony and raising a family together. I want a normal family life of happiness and love. I picture Anthony and I living in our farmhouse, raising children, and giving them the life I never had growing up. I see myself growing old with Anthony and getting buried next to him for eternity. I guess I want what everyone else wants, Dr. Lisa. That's where I see myself going in life and where I want to be."

"Cindy, those are pretty normal expectations. Last time we talked, you were telling me about how you would get back at your husband in your own ways and you gave me some examples of that. You also stated he became very abusive towards you. Can you give me some examples of his abusive behavior and do you think your provocations toward him brought out that behavior in him? Why do you think you're scared and paranoid at certain times and then have another side of you which gets angry and tries to provoke him?"

"Well, Dr. Lisa, you're right. There is one side of me that gets scared and worried and another side of me that gets angry and wants to make him pay. I guess I would put up with his behavior until it made me snap. Then he would put me in my place and knock me back down until the anger built up in me, then I would lash out again. It's a vicious, never-ending cycle. My relationship with James became very toxic. It was getting so bad, I was becoming terrified of him. I went from getting angry and taunting him to walking on eggshells so I wouldn't set him off. He gradually became more aggressive towards me. It started off with verbal abuse, then he started threatening me, and soon enough, it led to physical abuse. I was becoming afraid for my life."

"In what ways did he threaten you, Cindy?"

"At first, he became verbally abusive, threatening to throw me out of the house and telling me to go live with my parents again. He would threaten to fire Anthony and say he wouldn't allow him to come back, so I would rot in the house alone. Then he started drinking more and more whenever he was home and it started getting worse. The way he acted horrified me."

I almost started shivering, thinking about the things James did to me. I could feel the hair on my arms stand up. One night I was asleep on the couch and thought I heard a noise. I opened my eyes, rubbing them, and saw a dark shadow sitting in the chair across from me in the living room. Fear came over me and I froze. I was so scared. I slowly reached up in terror and turned the lamp on. It was James. He was sitting there, in the chair, just staring at me. He had his glass of whiskey in one hand and his other hand on the armrest of the chair, holding his gun and pointing it in my direction. I was so terrified, I almost cried. "What are you doing, James? And why do you have your gun?"

He took a sip of his whiskey while glaring at me. "Watching you sleep," he said.

"Why would you watch me sleep with your gun in your hand? Are you planning on doing something to me?"

"I just want to be clear about something, Cindy. You're my wife, and that means you belong to me. If I expect something out of you, you better damn well do it. I am the man of this house, and you better do as you're told."

I sat there in shock at what he just said. He got up out of the chair and walked over to me, still holding his gun and his drink. I started to cower and slouch down into the couch. He stared right at me with a stone cold face and said, "If you piss me off again, they will never find you. Do you understand me?"

I was shaking and almost could not speak when I said, "Yes, James, I understand."

He stumbled his way to his bedroom and shut the door. I didn't sleep all night. I went into the kitchen and got a knife to protect myself. I held it in my hand all night, unable to sleep.

"Cindy, that is horrifying. Did you report him to the authorities?"

"I couldn't. The police chief is James's best friend. Ethan would never believe James is capable of doing something like that."

"Did you tell anyone else about the incident?"

"No, who would I tell? If I told Vicky, then she would confront him and threaten him. She might even slap the shit out of him. Then James would come home and take it out on me. I didn't want to get Anthony involved out of fear he would do something to James and then James would either shoot him or fire him and I would never see Anthony again. He had me trapped and there wasn't anything I could do about it. I continued living in fear."

There was another incident when Anthony wasn't home. He stayed with his brother for the night to help him with something. I was asleep again, on the couch, and I felt my blanket get ripped off of me. James jumped on top of me and grabbed me by the hair, pinning me down. I screamed at him to get off of me.

> He put his hand around my throat. "Don't you forget you belong to me and I can do whatever I want to you," he said.

I was able to push him off of me, since he was drunk. He fell onto the floor, so I jumped up, ran out the back door and hid in the barn. He went to the door and started yelling to me, "You have to come back in at some point and when you do, I'm going to teach you a lesson."

I spent the night up in the hayloft, wrapped in a horse blanket to keep warm. When morning came, I listened for his car to leave before I went back into the house. I locked the doors and called Anthony, begging him to come home.

As soon as he got home, I wrapped my arms around him and made him promise to never leave me home alone again. He knew something was wrong. I told him James was drunk, and it scared me, so he wouldn't press me anymore about what happened. He promised to never leave me again and after that night, James and I avoided each other. I told him the following day if he ever came home drunk or started drinking at home, I would tell the police what he did to me.

Dr. Lisa asked, "What did he say when you confronted him about his behavior?"

"He looked at me like he didn't know what I was talking about and brushed it off."

His physical abuse stopped for a while. He got verbally abusive again later on. I was at the end of my rope with him. I was considering killing him at this point and knew if I walked into his room with a knife again, he wouldn't be alive by the time I walked back out of the room.

"Cindy, did his physical abuse stop because you said you were going to go to the police about what he did?"

"It was Anthony who put a stop to it," I said.

Dr. Lisa leaned forward in her chair with great curiosity. "How so?"

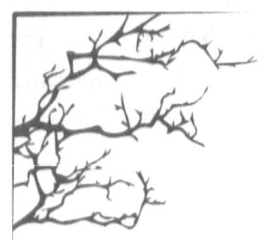

Chapter 17

James and I got into another heated argument one morning before he left for work. I was standing in front of him, poking my finger into his chest, and that's when he struck me in the face. He used the back of his hand and when he hit me, his knuckles caught me under the eye. It gave me a black eye. I had never had a black eye before and it hurt like hell. I ran to the couch and laid there crying while James walked out the door for work.

Later that day, Anthony came into the house looking for me. He found me still lying on the couch. He sat down beside me and put his hand on my arm. I turned my head further into my pillow so he wouldn't see what James did to me.

"What's wrong, Cindy? You haven't come outside to see me today. That's not like you at all. Did I upset you?"

"No, baby, everything is fine," I said.

He reached over and put his hand on my face to kiss me, and that's when I reacted. "Ow," I said. I turned to hide my face. He placed his fingers on my chin and turned my head to have a look at me. My eye was completely swollen shut at this point. It was black and blue and shiny. I couldn't see out of it and it was too sore to wipe away the watery tears that kept forming.

"What the hell is that? Do you have a black eye? How did you get a black eye? Did James do this to you? Please tell me that James did not do this to you," Anthony roared.

I cried. "Please, just let it go, Anthony. You don't know what he is capable of."

"I don't know what he is capable of? I can see clearly what he is capable of. He's capable of being a spineless coward and beating up on women. It's he who doesn't know what I am capable of! He has gone too far this time and I'm going to put a stop to it."

"Please, Anthony, let it go. If you don't, I'm afraid of what he might do to me."

Anthony went to the freezer and got an ice pack. "Here, put this on your eye. I will be right outside if you need anything," he said. He leaned down, kissed me on the forehead, and went out to the yard. For the rest of the day, Anthony never said a word. I could tell that it was eating him up inside. He was visibly angry. I have never seen him angry before. He is always so calm, even in times of trouble. I was so worried about what James might do when he finds out Anthony knows about what he did to me.

Later that night, Anthony and I were sitting on the couch together, watching television, when we saw the headlights of James's car pulling up to the house. As soon as the front door opened, Anthony got up and approached James as he was coming through the door. James looked shocked to see Anthony standing in front of him. Before James could say a word, Anthony punched him in the stomach so hard that James keeled over. I could hear his breath rush out of his lungs. James let out a loud groan and started coughing. His face turned blue and snot poured out of his nose. Anthony then grabbed him by the shoulder and pulled him up straight. I watched as Anthony took another swing at James. He hit him so hard in the face I could almost feel the thud that echoed through the house when his fist made contact with James's face. James went limp, fell back, and hit the floor hard.

"Cindy, can you please grab me a glass of cold water?"

"Sure," I said, still in shock at what was happening.

I walked over to the kitchen and got a glass of water from the sink. I handed it to Anthony, and he dumped it right on James's face. James woke up, still in shock. He squirmed on his back, away from Anthony. Anthony reached down and with one arm lifted James up off of the floor like it was nothing. Anthony put his hand around James's throat and pushed him up against the wall. "Where I come from, men don't put their hands on a woman. If I ever find out you so much as look at Cindy the wrong way, nevermind put a finger on her, I will beat you so hard, you will beg me to end your life. Do you understand what I am telling you?"

James nodded his head at Anthony, still shaking.

Anthony locked his eyes onto James. "Where is your gun, James?"

"In my trunk," James replied.

"Let's go get it."

Anthony walked James outside and made him open the trunk. Anthony reached in, got the gun, and put it in his waistband. Then he walked James back into the house.

"Your guns will be back in the closet the day I leave. Until then, I will keep them."

James muttered, "I could just fire you, Anthony, and make you leave."

Anthony stepped closer to James, getting only inches from his face. "Go ahead, fire me, James. I dare you to. The second you do, and I walk out that door, I'm taking Cindy with me. So if I were you, I would think long and hard about what comes out of your mouth next. And another thing, since you can't keep your hands to yourself, and I don't trust you, Cindy will be staying in the guest room with me from now on so I can keep her safe. I will not allow her to be out here on the couch, all alone and vulnerable, at the mercy of an abusive husband. Do you have a problem with that, James?" Anthony said, piercing James with his eyes. You could tell by the look on James's face he had a problem with it, but he would not admit it to Anthony. At least not to his face. "No, I don't have a problem with it, Anthony," James said, lowering his head.

"Good," Anthony said.

Anthony walked over to the couch, grabbed my pillow, wrapped his arm around me, and walked me to his bedroom, grabbing the rifle from the closet along the way. He shut the bedroom door and locked it, then placed the rifle under the mattress and the handgun in the nightstand drawer.

"You will be safe here with me, baby. I don't think he will put his hands on you again as long as I'm around." He pulled back the covers for me and I slid into his bed. He laid down beside me, holding me tight and comforting me until I fell asleep in his arms.

I can't express in words how good it made me feel when Anthony stood up for me. He made me feel safe, secure, and protected. To have someone who loved and cherished me and gave me purpose in life made my heart beat like never before. I have loved no one the way I love Anthony. That night gave me something new to focus on. I was now thinking harder about my future with Anthony and what we were going to do about it. I wanted to get as far away from James as I could. I wanted to talk to Anthony about where we were going to stay, so we can build our life together and start a family.

"Cindy, it's getting close to lunch, and I don't know about you, but I'm getting hungry. How about we wrap this up for today and start plugging away at it again tomorrow?"

"Okay, Dr. Lisa. See you tomorrow."

My lunch from the cafeteria soon arrived, and I was excited to get it. I've been snacking on things other than the occasional scrambled eggs, and now, in front of me, I have my first actual meal. I don't know if I would consider it proper food. I never eat like this so I can keep my figure, but I opted for chicken fingers, french fries and a piece of chocolate cake for dessert instead of my usual soup and salad when I'm not home.

It wasn't my preferred choice of food, but it was so comforting to be eating chicken fingers and fries. And the cake, wow, it was like a little slice of rich, decadent heaven on a plate. I understand why it takes such dedication and willpower to not eat unhealthy food every day, especially when unhealthy food tastes so delicious.

I thought more about the night Anthony stood up to James for me. He is such a good man to protect me the way he did. Even though my face was sore from James hitting me, and my eye was closed shut, I slept peacefully in Anthony's arms that night. I had nothing to fear because I knew I was under his safekeeping and it made me feel secure. What he did for me proved how much he loved me. He must have been so mad at James to do what he did. It shocked me when he told James I was going to be sleeping in the guest room with him from now on. It was a huge relief to not be sleeping on the couch anymore. I spent many nights afraid of James being right down the hall from me and wondering if this night would be the night he comes out from his room and hurts me, or worse, kills me.

Being in a locked room, naked in bed, with the love of my life every night was where I wanted to be. It's where I needed to be. James, knowing where I was, and there being nothing he could do about it, put me at ease. I could be in bed with my lover and not have to hide it anymore. Again, James's fault. He only continues to sabotage his life with me.

The next morning is when Anthony and I talked about what the future looked like for the both of us. We weighed all the pros and cons about how we were going to handle James. It was pretty clear we couldn't continue to live here if I was going to divorce James. It would be too risky and he would throw us both out. I was more concerned about James going off the deep end and killing us both once I handed him the divorce papers.

Anthony has been saving for years and said a down payment on a home won't be a problem. I also have some money in the bank since James has always paid for everything. My parents also gave me the remaining twenty thousand left over in my college fund to get myself an apartment after I finished school. We thought about looking for a house, but purchasing a home is a year-long process most times. Looking for a house would also be difficult. It would require a lot of traveling to look at places. We thought about getting an apartment but we can't get an apartment. What would we do with the horses?

The other problem is I don't want to give up my dream house if I don't have to. There has to be a way I can get rid of James without losing my home. How can I get rid of him? That is the first thing I need to figure out. The more I think about it, the more I realize the best way to handle it is to make James disappear for good. I can't involve Anthony, so I will have to do it by myself. Anthony would never allow me to kill someone, even if it was James. The more I thought about it, the more complicated it became. How can I explain his disappearance? Where do I kill him so there's no evidence? How do I kill him? How do I hide his body and where do I put it so no one finds it?

After the night Anthony beat up James, James didn't return home for almost three weeks. I don't know where he stayed, and I didn't dare ask him. The night he returned, he walked straight to his bedroom and shut the door. He barely spent any time at home after Anthony did that to him.

On the weekends, he would take off to wherever. I never knew when he would be home or if he was coming home. He never said a word to me. He acted like I didn't even exist. I just wish he would do us all a favor and never return. I wished every day he would crash his car and die or get killed in a robbery or something. Anything to get him out of my life. As I laid here thinking about everything, I started nodding off. I fell asleep.

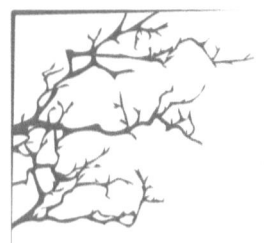

Chapter 18

Knock knock. "Open the door, it's me."

"Oh my gosh, James, what happened to you? Who did this to you? Did you get mugged? Come in and sit down. I will get some ice for your face."

"I don't want to talk about it."

"Here, put this on your face. Who did this to you, James?"

"Who the hell do you think? It was Anthony. Apparently, I'm not allowed to reprimand my psychotic wife without him stepping in to protect her."

"He did this to your face because of Cindy? Are you kidding me? I told you that you need to get rid of them! Why are they still alive?"

"Want to know the best part?"

"Do I really want to know, James?"

"She is now sleeping in his bedroom with him. Let that sink in. My wife is sleeping in bed with another man, in my fucking house. He did this to me and then took my wife down to his bedroom with him. He also took my guns from me. What the hell am I going to do now?"

"James, why didn't you kick him out of your house?"

"He dared me to fire him and kick him out. He said that when he walked out the door, he was taking Cindy with him."

"Why didn't you let him, you idiot? Then you would have gotten rid of them both and we could be together, James!"

"You know why I couldn't. Have you already forgotten? If she leaves and divorces me, she will get the house and I will have to pay her alimony. Is that what you want? Her and Anthony, living in our home, while I pay both of them to do just that?"

"James, we wouldn't be in this situation if you would have done what I told you to do already. I don't even know why the both of them are still breathing. You need to figure out a way to get rid of them and do it fast. Why don't you stay here for a few weeks until things blow over? Our bed misses you and I miss you."

"Then we will kill them. We will kill them. We... will... kill... them! Hahahahahahahaha. You're going to die, Cindy! Die... Die... Die!"

"No!" I screamed as I jumped up. Oh shit! Another nightmare? Why am I having these nightmares? I don't remember ever having them before my accident. It must be because of my brain injury? Or maybe it's the drugs they have me on? I wonder if there is anything the doctor can give me to make them stop? I put on the television to keep my mind off of things until I fell back asleep again.

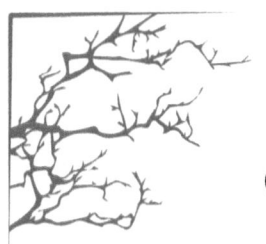

Chapter 19

"Hello, James."

"Hi, Dr. Lisa."

"Thank you for spending the time to come in today and talk to me. It's important I get your point of view on Cindy's behavior and what she's been telling me. I know you're both going through a difficult time right now, but I think the time to get help for either of you is now, while you both have the resources available. I'm here to discuss Cindy, but I would like to get some information on your background, if you don't mind."

"That's fine. Anything to get Cindy the help she needs."

"Tell me a little about your childhood. Was it normal? Were you raised by both of your parents? Did you have a lot of friends growing up?"

"I had a good upbringing. Both my parents raised me in the home. They were very loving and never fell short of providing for me. I had a ton of friends and I was very popular in school."

"So, James, life has always been pretty normal for you, I assume?"

"Yes, things have always been normal in my life until I met Cindy."

"And how did things change when you met her?"

"My life started getting complicated. I met her in college and our relationship started off great, but her behavior put a strain on our life together. It gradually got worse as the years went by. At first I noticed some strange behaviors. She would go into some type of trance. Sometimes it would last for hours. When she came out of it, she wouldn't remember what she was doing. I would also catch her talking to herself throughout the day. It caused an argument between us one time and that's when she told me about her childhood and Brenda. I thought it was strange to be in college and still have an imaginary friend."

Dr. Lisa asked, "So why did you decide to marry her if you knew she was having these problems?"

"At that point in our relationship, I was already in love with her and I couldn't bring myself to break her heart. Also, I thought she would get better and grow out of it now that she wasn't alone anymore. I mean, who has make-believe friends this late in life? I suggested to her all the time that she should talk to someone and get some help. All it did was agitate her and get her furious at me."

"James, are you aware Cindy makes up people to fill certain voids in her life? She speaks a lot about a man named Anthony. How familiar are you with this person?"

"To be honest, Doc, I hoped that after suffering a brain injury, she would have forgotten about him."

Dr. Lisa's eyes widened as she leaned forward in her chair. "I'm confused. Are you saying he does exist?" she asked.

"Yes, he exists, but he isn't real. He only exists in her mind. He is another imaginary friend she created."

"Oh, so he is another person who Cindy has made up?"

"Yes."

"James, what about Brenda? Does she still mention her?"

"No, I believe Brenda got replaced once Anthony came into the picture. After Anthony, I never heard about Brenda again."

"How did her relationship with Anthony affect your marriage?"

"It affected my marriage severely. At least with Brenda, I only had to deal with it seldomly. With Anthony, I have to deal with it every day. She replaced me with him. She has a very sick obsession with Anthony and it became dangerous, not only for her but for me as well."

"When did Cindy bring Anthony into her life? Was it when you worked long hours and your job expected you to leave town for weeks at a time? It would make sense that her being alone a lot would be a trigger for her. It's the reason she felt the need to have Brenda in her life to begin with."

"Is that what she told you? I work a regular nine-to-five job, Monday through Friday, and I am home every night. I have never had to travel for work and I can get you all my time sheets if need be. Most of the time, while I was home, she wouldn't acknowledge me at all. I didn't exist to her when she was having her delusions. I would try to talk to her and it didn't phase her one bit. She treated me like I was invisible and, honestly; I don't think I was on her mind at all. The only time she acknowledged me was to fight with me."

"So, James, she just went on with her life everyday like you weren't even there? Can you give me an example of how she would behave?"

"One time, when she was in her 'other state of mind', as I would call it, she took off for a couple of days by herself. I overheard her talking to Anthony one Friday night that she was planning a trip with him to go three hours away for a weekend getaway. I didn't know she would actually take off. She got up early in the morning and grabbed a bag she packed the night before. On her way out the door, I asked her where she was going and she just walked right by me like I wasn't even there. Then she did something I never expected her to do. She threw her bag into my car and took off. I found it strange because she has never driven my car before and she just jumped in that day and took it. Cindy doesn't even have a driver's license."

"I was worried about her and what she was planning on doing, so I had a friend come pick me up. He let me borrow his car, so I followed her to where she was going. She made a couple of stops on the way, ate at a diner, and spent the night in a motel by herself. The following morning, she left and drove back home. I returned my friend's car, and he dropped me back off the same night. I just thought the whole thing was weird. After that, I started hiding my car keys so she wouldn't take off again when she was having one of her spells."

"How often was Cindy interacting with Anthony? How much time did she spend having these delusions?"

"At first, it didn't seem to be as frequent. I think she was trying to hide it. I would watch her sometimes and catch her outside, standing at the fence or in the barn carrying on a conversation with nobody but herself. She was always looking over her shoulder to see if I was around. It wasn't long before her demeanor changed and started getting worse. She got more brazen and aggressive towards me. She started a fight with me one night out of nowhere and demanded that she sleep on the couch. I will not lie. It made me angry, but I was beginning to not trust her and with good reason."

"James, Cindy thinks you are trying to kill her. Is there any reason she would think that?"

"It's because I started carrying my gun around with me."

"Why did you feel the need to have a gun with you?"

"There was one night I was asleep in bed. I will never forget it. Cindy was sleeping on the couch at this point in time. I was sound asleep and even though I was asleep; I had a sudden bad feeling in my gut that woke me up. As soon as I rolled over, I saw Cindy standing at the side of my bed. She tried to hide a knife she was holding and then ran out of the room. I laid in bed all night, awake and terrified. From that point on, I always kept my gun on me for my safety. I didn't know what her plan was, but I felt that my life was in danger."

"Did Cindy continue to get worse as time went on?"

"I think so. She continued to change. She would start doing weird things like sleeping naked, walking around the house naked, and spending time outside in the nude. Her obsession with Anthony got worse every day, and her aggression toward me also intensified. After I caught her standing over me with a knife, I started keeping to myself. Cindy scared me and I feared for my life. I wasn't sure what she was capable of doing. I felt like it was a losing battle. The more I tried to interact with her, the more she acted like I wasn't there. The more I avoided her, the more she would act out for attention."

"James, Cindy said she would do things to provoke you. Did she intentionally do things to upset you?"

"She did a good job of getting under my skin. It took a lot of self control to keep my anger at bay. I had to remind myself that she was sick, and that I loved her. It was a hard pill to swallow, knowing the woman I loved and married, is not who I thought she was. I wanted to get her help, but I didn't know how to."

"What things would she do to 'get under your skin' as you said?"

"One thing she would do was try to make me jealous of Anthony. It wasn't good enough for her to be spending every waking moment with her imaginary lover. She had to throw it in my face as well. Every time she would mention his name, she would do little things like smile, sigh or giggle. She would pretend to have sex with him just to get me angry."

"I'm confused, James. How would she pretend to have sex with a man who doesn't exist?"

"It started with Cindy dressing herself up in the most provocative clothing she had, which were very short dresses. She would ask me if I had seen Anthony and then disappear to go look for him. After a while, she would come back with her hair a mess and looking worn out. Then she would come see me to tell me she found him, and to let me know he took care of her. She got so bad when we argued she would strip off her clothes right in front of me. Then she would look at me and say, 'I need to go find Anthony.' Then she would walk outside or down to the guest bedroom and wouldn't come back for hours. It didn't bother me as bad as it should have. I mean, it would be ridiculous to get jealous of a man who didn't exist. However, it was annoying having to put up with it. I started pulling away from her. I was tired of dealing with the constant dysfunction. It was becoming exhausting."

"James, you mentioned Cindy started becoming aggressive toward you. Her standing over you with a knife while you slept is pretty serious. What other things would she do?"

"She would throw things at me, shove me or threaten me. She thought I was having an affair and thought I wanted to kill her and Anthony."

"Were you having an affair, James?"

"Oh gosh, no. I married Cindy because I love her and couldn't bring myself to break her heart, so why would I have an affair and do just that to her? What I want is my wife back. I want her to get help and to be normal so we can live a normal life together."

"Did Cindy's aggression toward you get worse over time? She says you're the one who became physically abusive towards her. She mentioned you gave her a black eye once?"

"Of course she would say something like that. It's typical that she would blame me. Yes, it got worse over time. The closer she got to Anthony, the worse she would behave towards me. Cindy is the one who became physically abusive and she would even blame her own injuries on me for whatever reason."

"How so, James?"

"As far as the black eye, one day she was running through the yard, yelling to Anthony and she tripped and hit her face on the fence. I got her inside and gave her some ice to put on her eye. She had a pretty good black eye from the fall. We were out of aspirin, so I went into town to pick some up. When I got back home, I found her in the bathroom, looking into the mirror and talking to Anthony. She was telling him I did this to her and wanted to know what he was going to do about it. I asked her if she was okay and that's when she screamed at me and chased me down the hall into the living room. I tried to get out the door as she picked up the flashlight from the counter and smashed me right in the face with it."

"She started screaming at me, telling me I will never put my hands on her again. She said from now on she was sleeping in the guest bedroom with Anthony so he can keep her safe from me. I begged her not to and told her I wanted her to come back to our bedroom and she wouldn't listen. She grabbed her pillow off of the couch and went down to the guest bedroom."

"She gave me two black eyes that day. It was hard to come up with a story to tell people at work and I was so upset over the whole incident, I didn't bother going home for a few weeks. I just didn't have it in me to face her, and I was drained and exhausted from putting up with it. I was considering therapy for myself."

"I did the only thing that I could think of doing. I just started avoiding her and letting her live in her fantasy. I gave up and realized I no longer had a marriage and it is what it is at this point. It wasn't hard to ignore her. She never came to me for anything other than to get under my skin, which I learned to brush off. I spent most of my time at home in my office, avoiding her."

"Anthony consumed her days from the time she woke until the time she went to bed. I stopped trying to help her. I think it's what she wanted. Once she realized I had no interest in her, it made her a little more comfortable to be around me. As long as I didn't interfere with her delusional affair, she seemed to be happy for the time being."

"It didn't take long before she started going downhill again. She started acting paranoid around me. I didn't know what was going on until I heard through the door a conversation she was having with herself. She said she had to get rid of me somehow and she talked about how she didn't want to give up the house. I guess she was worried that I would try to take it from her.

She was concerned I would kill her and Anthony if she tried to divorce me. She convinced herself that I wanted her dead, and she needed to kill me first before I got to her and Anthony. I felt helpless at this point and I couldn't understand why the woman I loved would want to hurt me and want me dead. I gave her everything she wanted, a marriage and her dream house. I took her away from her parents, who were destroying her emotionally and did everything I could for her. In the end, there was nothing I could do to help her. I'm thinking there is no hope for Cindy."

"James, I know how difficult it is to deal with someone who is sick. These disorders are serious and people need to get treatment before they end up hurting somebody. There are ways to get help, and I will discuss it with you later. I don't want you feeling hopeless."

"I get it, Dr. Lisa. I just don't think I can feel safe about her coming home yet. At least not until she gets some help. Her only concern when she woke up, the day I visited her here, was Anthony. She tried to act like she was just confused, but I could tell she was sincerely concerned about him and didn't care about how bad her brain injury was or how it might affect her. She only wanted to know where Anthony was. What if her brain injury made her hallucinations and delusions worse? How do we know? If she is worse, then she might kill me when she gets out. How do I deal with that? How do I know if she is worse off now? I just want my wife back and I want the woman I fell in love with. I want the real Cindy."

"James, that is why it is important you and I have this conversation so I can evaluate whether her condition has worsened or improved since her injury. I have been speaking to Cindy quite a bit to get her take on things and now that I know from you how she has acted over the years, I can make a judgment on whether her condition has declined or improved."

"As of right now, Dr. Lisa, what is your professional opinion on what should be done?"

"I think Cindy is suffering from a multitude of mental illnesses that require immediate attention. Things like split personality disorder, paranoid schizophrenia and some other issues. I think if she continues in the state that she is in, she will wind up hurting herself or someone else. She is going to need medication and therapy for the rest of her life. This is something that is going to require effort from everyone involved in her life, especially you, James. And if you're not up to the task, then we need to explore other options to get Cindy the help she needs."

"Dr. Lisa, I'm not sure what I want to do at this point. Her condition has sucked the life right out of me. I'm not sure if I want to spend the rest of my life living in fear of the person whom I married."

"James, if you decide to move forward with a life which still involves your wife, I would recommend you also get counseling. You're going to need it, not just for Cindy, but for yourself, James. Another thing I would recommend you do before she returns home is to get rid of anything unsafe she could use. Lock up your kitchen knives or anything sharp. Get rid of your guns so she can't ever get access to them, things such as that, to keep you both safe."

"It's frustrating, Dr. Lisa. I put so much into her, so I'm going to need some time to think about things because I don't know what I want to do right now. I gave her everything she has ever wanted, and I was always there for her. Now it's become too much for me, I think. I'm going to need more time to process everything before I make any permanent decisions."

"That's understandable, James. I'm here if you need to talk. My number is on the card I gave you. I will try to help the both of you as much as I can."

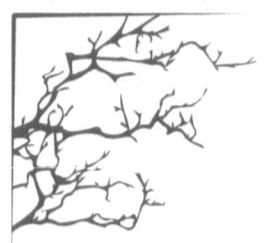

Chapter 20

"Cindy, I have some good news," the nurse said, walking into my room.

I perked up. "What news?"

"The doctor feels like you are stable enough to go home, so we will release you in a few days."

A rush of excitement flowed through me as I smiled from ear to ear. "Are you kidding me? Are you being serious right now?" I asked.

"As much as I enjoy having you around, it's time for you to go, girl. Are you excited to be getting out of here?"

"Oh, my gosh, you don't even know how excited I am."

Then she gave me a smile and left. I wanted to jump up and down. I was ecstatic to go find Anthony and get back to my life. I don't even care where we will stay at this point while I divorce James. I'm so close to being free again, I can smell his perfect scent and taste his lips. I've been dreaming of the day I can find solace in his warm embrace again.

Time stood still for the next couple of days. It was torture. It would feel like an hour had gone by, only to realize that only ten minutes have passed, every time I glanced up at the clock.

The only thing I dreaded was going home to James. Where else would I go? I guess I will have to deal with it until I find my love again. Once I find Anthony, we can run off together. I'm sure we can find somewhere to go until the divorce is finalized. Then we can get married and we can live happily ever after.

The morning of my release came. I didn't sleep at all. I got up early to wait for the nurse to bring in whatever clothes or personal items they had of mine. I spent a lot of time in front of the bathroom mirror trying to look my best, just in case I ran into Anthony right away. I washed my face and tried to fix my hair a dozen times. The backside of my head must look horrible, I thought. I'm sure it bothers me more than it would bother Anthony. He loves me no matter what I look like.

I took off my hospital gown to check myself from head to toe. It's been a while since I saw myself naked. I expected to be more on the slender side and figured I would have lost weight since being here. I have eaten so little. It almost seems like I might have put on a couple of pounds, which is fine. The last thing I want to do is lose my hourglass figure and start looking skinny.

I went back to bed after pacing back and forth in my room for a while. I was having a hard time withholding my excitement. I was becoming anxious. Then, there was a soft knock on my door and the door began to open. This is it, I thought, this is what I've been waiting for. As soon as I saw who it was, my heart sank, and I felt faint. Dr. Lisa came into my room and she had two of the hospital security guards with her.

"What is going on, Dr. Lisa? Why are you here and why is there security with you?"

"Cindy, they are here for my safety as well as yours. There is something we need to discuss. I don't feel you are ready to be released, so I am committing you to a ten-day program, for further evaluation, in our Behavioral Health Department."

"What? No, you can't do this to me! I'm supposed to get out today so I can go find Anthony. Why are you doing this to me? Why?" I started crying, and I could feel the rage building inside of me. I jumped off of the bed and ran at her, tackling her to the ground. The guards pulled me off of her, threw me down on the bed, holding me down, while they yelled for the nurse. I kept squirming and trying to get back up. "I'm going to kill you for doing this to me! You have no right to do this! I've done nothing wrong! Please! Please stop. I don't deserve this. I'm begging you."

Dr. Lisa picked herself up off of the floor and shuffled out of the room while a nurse came running in. I felt a stinging pinch, then after a couple of minutes, things got blurry. I blacked out.

I woke up in an unfamiliar room. It was a somewhat normal room. The bed is a twin sized bed made up with blankets that didn't look like your typical hospital blankets. There is a nightstand next to the bed with a lamp on it and a bookshelf with a few books. Also, a dresser with empty drawers and a bathroom with a shower in it. It was almost like a motel room. The door to the room was closed. I walked over to the door thinking it's just a room they were keeping me locked in, so I reached down and turned the knob. It surprised me to find the door unlocked. I opened it and peered out into the hall. The hall had other doors to rooms I assume are just like mine. I started walking down the hall to see where I was. I made it to a nurse's work station where a man was sitting.

"Hello, Cindy, I'm Nathan. How are you feeling?"

"I'm a little groggy and I don't feel so well. Where am I?"

"You're in the Behavioral Health Wing of the hospital."

"I don't want to be here. I want to leave. Can I leave?"

"No, you can't leave. The exit doors are locked. The good news is we can only hold you here for ten days, so just take it one day at a time and you will be out before you know it. Here, come with me and I will show you around. We have a room with games and a television to help pass the time, a kitchen area with stocked cabinets and a fridge in case you get hungry and want a snack between meals. This is the room where we have group meetings. You don't have to attend, but we recommend you do."

"One rule we have, and it's a big one, is that you don't go into anyone else's room or down this hallway over here. This is the men's hall. Girls aren't allowed down there and guys aren't allowed down the girls' hall. There is always someone at the workstation and staff is available twenty-four hours a day. Your therapist will talk to you a few times in the next week. Do you have any questions for me?"

"No, I'm still pretty tired. I think I'm going to lie down and try to sleep some more."

I found my way back down the hallway towards my room, and as I walked in, I got startled by what I saw; I jumped. There was a girl sitting on the side of my bed and she didn't look like she belonged here.

She isn't wearing any hospital clothing and has black leather boots laced up tight. Fishnet stockings adorned her legs up to her short black skirt. She had on a punk rock tee shirt and a leather jacket. She was wearing bright red lipstick with a silver hoop lip piercing. Her hair was black and pulled back behind her ears. Once I heard her snarky tone say, "Well, well, well, look who shows up after all this time." I knew who it was. Her voice was so familiar and unforgettable. She sounded older, but I would never forget that voice.

"Oh, my gosh. Brenda, is that you?"

"Of course it's me. It's about time you showed up. I thought you left me for good and I would never see you again, Cindy."

"You look so different, Brenda."

"I'm older now, Cindy. You don't look the same either."

"So, why are you here in my room?"

She took a long, good look at me. "Cindy, we need to have a serious conversation. I don't know if you're aware of what is happening to you, but we need to figure this out before it's too late." She reached into her jacket pocket and pulled out a pack of cigarettes. She took one out and placed it into her mouth.

"Brenda, are you crazy? You can't smoke cigarettes here. It's a hospital. Don't even light that."

She put her cigarette back in the packaging. "Fine, Cindy, have it your way." She glanced around the room. "I've noticed your life has been going to shit without me. See what happens when we stop talking. I thought you would have figured it out by now. You need me and have always needed me. You think just because you have Anthony now, you don't need me anymore? Look how that's turned out for you."

"I'm sorry, Brenda. I'm preoccupied with Anthony because I love him so much. It hurts to be away from him."

"Cindy, look at where you are now. Locked up. That's what happens when you turn your back on your best friend. I shouldn't even be here, but I am because I care about you. Every time you needed me, I was right there for you. I was there with you right from the start when your asshole parents left you alone all the time. I can leave if that's what you want."

"No, Brenda, please don't leave. I need you. You are right, I never should have stopped hanging out with you. It's great to see you. I don't have anyone. I'm just stuck in this hospital and I'm losing all hope."

"I know. That's why I'm here. Why don't you get some sleep and I will be back to see you tonight so we can figure this out? I got something I need to take care of right now."

"Okay, Brenda. It was good seeing you again. I have missed you. See you tonight." It was strange to see Brenda all grown up, but it was comforting to see a familiar face when I have nobody. Brenda was right about one thing. Every time I needed her, she was always there for me, and at a time when I have no one, she is here for me again.

I curled up on my bed with no intention of getting back up. If I could sleep the next ten days away, I would. Waiting three days for my release was too long before. Now I have to make it ten more days until I see Anthony. I don't know how I'm going to make it. I fell asleep and then I woke to the sound of Brenda.

"Cindy, get up. Come on, wake up."

"Ugh, what time is it?"

"It's midnight. I told you I would be back, so here I am."

"Yeah, but at midnight, Brenda?"

"There's no time like the present. Move over and give me some room to lie down as well." Brenda stretched out next to me and we both lied here staring at the ceiling together until she said, "What are we going to do about that asshole husband of yours and his girlfriend? They are destroying your life and your happiness."

"What do you think I'm going to do? I'm going to divorce him and marry Anthony. You should already know this."

"You're going to divorce him? How pathetic is that? The guy ruins your life, threatens to kill Anthony and you're just going to divorce him? I thought I taught you better than that? You need to stand up for yourself. Stop being such a pussy, Cindy. You let your parents walk all over you, as well. Now this prick is doing the same thing and you're just going to divorce him? I don't know why I bother with you sometimes," she said.

"I'm sorry things are so easy for you, Brenda, but I'm not you. You're tough and don't take any shit from people. I can't just take someone's life. It's not so easy. I tried already and failed. I want James dead and I almost killed him, but I couldn't go through with it."

"I already know you can't do it. You're pathetic, Cindy. Just like the night I handed you a knife and told you to go take care of your parents on the night they yelled at you. You couldn't do it then either, so why would I expect you to do it now? I don't know why I keep dealing with you. At some point, you need to grow up and put on your big girl pants, Cindy. I can't keep holding your hand for the rest of your life."

"What would you suggest I do, Brenda? I'm locked up in here right now. It's not like I can get up and walk out the door."

"You need to escape. If you get out of here, then you can go take care of James and that bitch he is with. Just think about what he is doing to you. You're locked up in here, while he is at home right now, in your house, having sex with some woman in your bed while you're rotting away in here. I bet he laughs about you every day he kisses her on the way out the door. You're a fool, Cindy. You should have killed him the night you had the chance. If I were you, I would have killed the bastard as soon as he started leaving you home alone and treating you the same way your parents treated you. You're better than this."

"You're right Brenda. I should have taken care of him already. He's the reason I'm here. I bet he went crying to that douchebag doctor and convinced her to put me in here. Tomorrow I will try to get out."

"Good girl, Cindy. I will come and check on you again soon. Don't let me down this time. I'm counting on you."

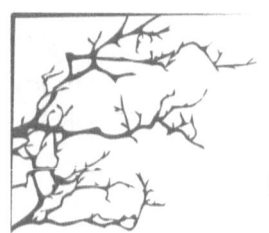

Chapter 21

I spent the following day trying to look for ways to get out of here. None of the windows were open and even if they did open, it would be quite a fall. I'm not sure what floor I am on, but it's a few floors up from the ground. There is a door at the end of each hallway, but they are locked and never used. They are emergency doors that will only open in an actual emergency, like a fire or something. The only door that has access is the entrance next to the nurse's workstation.

I strolled around the place just to get an idea of what I was dealing with and to think about what options I have. I even attended one of the group sessions to get a feel for the other people locked up here. Maybe I can befriend another person to help me, I thought. The group session made me very irritated. I couldn't believe I was even here after witnessing the other patients. I mean, these are very sick people that have some serious issues going on. It actually scares me to be locked up here with them. Why would I even be in a place like this? I am not crazy and if I was, I'm not as crazy as these people are. I feel insulted and disgusted.

I realized there was only one way in and out of this place, and it's the entrance door. I sat in the kitchen area across from the nurse's station for the next two days and kept track of when the staff would come and go. My best chance would be during the morning shift change at nine o'clock. If I hang out by the door at the workstation, then I might have time to run through it.

With my feeble escape plan, I went back to my room to lie in bed and pass the time sleeping. I'm going to need all the energy I can get if I'm going to be on foot and running all day tomorrow. I was lying here thinking about how I was going to get home, when Brenda appeared.

"So, you're going to do it? You're going to escape?"

"Yes, I'm getting out of here, one way or another."

"Good, make me proud, Cindy. Don't forget to take care of James and the bitch he is with when you get home."

"I won't forget."

"Okay, I will check back in with you tomorrow."

Then, just like that, she disappeared. Wow, she really wants me to kill James and his lover. I mean, I want them dead too, but the only reason I want to be out of here is to be with Anthony. Right now, he is my only priority.

I got up early the next morning, took a shower, and ate a bowl of cereal. It was almost time for the morning shift change, so I went to the workstation and started a conversation with the nurse. I asked him a bunch of silly questions and did my best to entertain him until I saw the door open and a man step through. Before the door could close, I ran at him so hard that I knocked him to the ground on my way through. As I took off down the hall, I could hear the nurse from the workstation yelling at people to catch me. I looked over my shoulder and he was in pursuit of me. I ran down several hallways, pushing people out of my way and searching for an elevator. I got to the elevator and hit the button several times. The door didn't open. I had no time to wait as they were closing in on me.

I panicked and took off running again. There was a stairwell sign at the end of the hall, so I took off in that direction. I made it through the door. My instinct was to run down the stairs, but I knew that's where they would expect me to go, so I ran up a couple of flights of stairs to a different floor.

I stepped through the door, looking around to make sure no one was chasing after me. I kept my head down while I walked the halls, trying to find the elevator. Then my heart stopped as soon as I heard a voice call out to me. "Excuse me, can I help you? What are you doing on this floor?" I pretended I didn't hear her, but she caught up with me. Her clothes gave it away that she worked in the hospital. She was wearing green scrubs and had a work badge clipped to her front shirt pocket. I looked up at her and said the first thing that came to mind.

"Sorry, I am lost. I must have gotten off on the wrong floor. I was trying to make it to my room, but then I realized I wasn't on my floor. Is there any way you can show me where the elevator is?"

"Sure, just follow me," she said.

We walked down a couple of hallways right to the elevator. "Thank you so much. I will pay attention to the floor I need to get off of this time."

She smiled and said, "You're welcome."

As soon as the elevator doors opened, I rushed in. I hit the ground floor button, then continued to hit the door button, waiting for them to close. My heart was racing, and I panicked the entire way down, hoping it wouldn't stop on any other floor, especially the floor I just came from. I eventually made it to the ground floor and watched as the doors opened. "Shit!" I screamed. Once the doors opened enough, two hospital security guards rushed in and grabbed me. They brought me back to the wing I just attempted to flee from as I was kicking and screaming the whole way.

"Stop, let go of me! I don't belong here and I want to leave! Please stop." I started losing it. I couldn't see from all the tears that were pouring out of my eyes. "Anthony, where are you?" I cried out.

They brought me straight to my room and locked me in. Brenda was already sitting on my bed. I knew how disappointed she would be in my failed attempt to escape. I wasn't in the mood for a lecture, but I was going to get one, regardless.

"Are you kidding me, Cindy? You failed? You were so close to getting out of here and you fucked it up?" she said.

"I don't want to hear it, Brenda. I'm not in the mood and since when do you tear me down? You have always supported me and now you're treating me just like the others do. I don't need your shit right now," I yelled.

"You don't need my shit, Cindy? Since when do you talk to me like that? I have done nothing but stand up for you, but there comes a point when you need to stand up for yourself. You need to get your act together. We used to be very close until you met your precious Anthony. Then you stopped having me around. As a matter of fact, I'm sick of this guy getting in the way of our friendship. You have two choices. Get rid of him or get rid of me. I won't come second to some no good asshole lover of yours."

"What did you just say to me, Brenda?"

"You heard me, Cindy. Did I stutter? It's me or that no good asshole of yours."

"You're going to regret calling my Anthony names! Get out, Brenda, and never come back! Do you hear me? Get the fuck out, now!"

Brenda stood there composed and unaffected by my screaming. She pulled out a cigarette, lit it and blew a big cloud of smoke into my face, causing me to fan it away. She said, calmly, "You think Anthony is so great Cindy? Where is he now? Has he come to get you out of here? No, he hasn't. Oh, but look, Brenda is here when you have nobody. I'm tired of being such a sucker. If you want me gone, fine, I will leave. Have fun figuring this out on your own from now on."

Then Brenda turned around and vanished into thin air.

I kept screaming and throwing anything I could pick up in my room. Once I calmed down and realized how badly I trashed my room, the realization of Brenda being gone hit me. I knew she was gone for good this time. Something inside of me told me so. I could just feel it. It felt good to know she was never coming back, and I felt at peace with myself about it. I didn't want her back. I want Anthony. Now all I need to do is get rid of the other trash in my life so I can be with him.

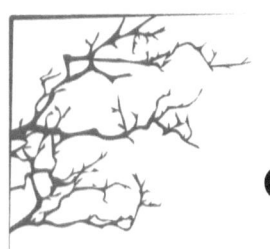

Chapter 22

The following morning, the staff came to get me for my meeting with Dr. Lisa. They brought me to a small room with just a few chairs, a low table and a couple of end tables.

Dr. Lisa was already sitting in the chair closest to the door. She looked unfazed at the sight of me. I wanted to punch her right in the face, but I didn't.

"Good morning, Cindy. How are you doing?" she asked cheerfully.

The sound of her voice was like nails on a chalkboard. I detested and despised her voice. I thought about wrapping my hands around her throat and squeezing until she shut her mouth permanently. All I could do was sit here and stare at her like I wanted to kill her because, realistically, I did want to kill her.

"Cindy?" she said in a calm voice.

I turned my head and ignored her. Just the sight of her face made me sick. I can't believe she would lock me away in here. When I looked away, I noticed a painting hanging on the wall. It was beautiful. It's a painting of wildflowers. All different colored ones. It reminded me of home.

As I continued to stare at it, I remembered the day I picked some wildflowers for Anthony. It surprised him and made us both smile.

It was a gorgeous day outside. The sun was shining, and the sky was bright blue. The temperature was perfect. I figured it was a good day to deal with my vegetable garden. I have neglected it for the last week and some plants are overdue for picking.

Anthony wasn't too far from me. He was painting the fence close by. He waved and smiled at me as I made my way over to the greenhouse to get my supplies I needed to harvest some vegetables. I put on my gardening gloves, grabbed my pruning shears and basket, then went out to pick the plants. I inspected the mess of a garden that was taking over the landscape. As I walked through the rows of plants, trying to decide where I was going to start, something caught my eye. It was a bouquet of vivid colors scattered over a small area in the field. I went over to get a closer look. It was a variety of wildflowers in full bloom. I couldn't believe how pretty they were. They almost glistened in the sun as they swayed in the light breeze blowing across the field.

I looked over at Anthony and saw how beautiful he was, standing there, sweaty and glistening in the sun as well. I decided I was going to pick some flowers for my love. It's not common for a woman to give a man flowers, but he deserved to get something as beautiful as he is.

I crouched down in the flower patch, trying not to trample or crush any of the flowers. There were so many of them, it was hard to choose which ones I wanted to pick. I soon gathered enough flowers to make a hefty bunch and started walking toward Anthony. As I approached him, he stopped what he was doing and put his attention on me.

"Those are some beautiful flowers you have there. They are almost as beautiful as you, my gorgeous lady. Did you pick those for the house?"

I looked up at him, batting my eyelashes. "No, I picked them for you. I just wanted to show you how much I appreciate you and love you."

His face brightened up, and he smiled as I handed them to him. He took the flowers while admiring them at the same time. "Wow, Cindy. I've never gotten flowers before. This is the sweetest gift anyone has ever given me. I will put them on the table in the barn so I can see them every time I go in there. I have a jar in the tack room I can use. Come here and give me a hug."

I stepped closer to him. He wrapped his arm around me and pulled me close. He kissed me on the forehead and said, "Thank you. I love you so much. Which flower is your favorite?"

"My favorite are the daisies. I will make sure I keep replacing them with fresh ones for you as they die off." I kissed him on the cheek and said, "I love..."

Then I got interrupted. "Cindy, wake up!" Then the loud clap of Dr. Lisa's hands made me come back to reality. I was dreaming of Anthony, and of course, she had to ruin it. Just like she ruins my life every day with her annoying presence.

"Cindy, you were in a daze again. I need you to talk to me. Is there anything I can do for you?"

I gave her an evil stare and said, "Yes, Lisa, you can fuck off!"

The look of shock on her face was priceless, and I enjoyed it very much.

"Cindy, I will not sit here and get treated like this. I will not tolerate it, so I'm going to leave and we will try again another time."

She got up from her chair and turned toward the door. I don't know what came over me, but what I did next was impulsive. I jumped up behind her and put her in a choke hold with my arm. She shrieked and dropped her notepad on the floor.

"Open the door, Lisa!" I commanded her.

I pushed her toward the door so she could reach the knob. She reluctantly opened the door while I forced her into the hall. There were already two staff members running towards us. I squeezed tighter around her neck as she tried to struggle, knocking her glasses to the floor.

I moved closer to the entrance door, with Lisa still in my grasp.

"Let her go, Cindy. There is no reason for this. You're hurting her," one of the staff said.

I shouted back at him, "If you don't let me out of here, I will snap her neck!" I pulled up on her neck even more this time, tightening my hold. Lisa was frantically grabbing at my arms and struggling to breathe.

"I will kill her. I will seriously fucking kill her if you don't let me out!"

More staff were coming to Lisa's aid and started surrounding me. As I stood there with Dr. Lisa at my mercy, I looked for a way through the crowd of people forming around me. Then I felt a quick sharp pinch in my shoulder while I was looking in the other direction. I spun around to see what it was, and I saw one of the staff standing there, holding an empty needle syringe. After a few more minutes of struggling with Lisa, I felt weak. The room started moving around and I could no longer hold my weight up. I fell back into the wall and everything went dark.

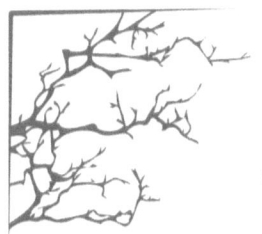

Chapter 23

"Cindy, wake up. Are you awake?"

I felt someone tapping my leg. I could barely open my eyes because of the stupor I'm in from the drugs they administered to me. I tried to look up to see who it was. There, standing at the side of my bed, was Nathan, the nurse who works at the front desk. He said, "Come on Cindy, get up. It's your lucky day."

"Leave me alone. I'm too tired to deal with anyone right now."

"Okay, if you're too tired to go home, then I can come back and wake you up later."

What did I just hear? Did he say that I was going home? I woke up as much as I could, while I jumped up from my bed. "Are you messing with me? This is not funny. Don't mess with me like this," I said.

"No, I'm not messing with you, Cindy. I wouldn't joke about something like this. I'm being serious," he said.

I thought I was dreaming. I looked at him, still expecting him to burst out laughing, and asked, "Yeah, but how? Why would they just release me now?"

He sat down next to me on the bed and said, "There has been a change to our policy because of legalities. We can no longer keep people against their will who are over the age of eighteen without a court order. We can only keep minors with parental consent against their will. So, what this means is, if you don't want to stay, you can sign yourself out and leave. I put your personal belongings over there on the dresser, along with a new pair of scrubs for you. Your clothes have blood on them and it looks like they cut your shirt off of you. Whenever you are ready, you come see me. I will have the paperwork ready and I will go over it with you."

He stood up from the bed and walked out of the room. I couldn't believe what I just heard and I still don't believe it. I looked over at the bags sitting on the dresser, realizing he wasn't lying to me, so I checked to see what was in them. One bag had my pair of cowgirl boots and the other bag had my tattered clothes in it. It seems like I haven't seen my clothes in forever. Being able to touch them felt like my first actual glimpse of freedom. I rushed to put them on.

"What?" My shorts don't fit? I can't even button them. How did I put on this much weight? I barely eat. I put on the scrubs and went to get myself out of here once and for all.

Nathan had the paperwork waiting on the counter for me when I got to the workstation. He slid it over to me and said, "Let me explain these papers so you understand what you're signing."

"No, thank you, Nathan, but I don't care what they say. Just show me where to sign so I can leave."

He flipped the top papers over and pointed to a blank line on the page. I picked up the pen and scribbled my name like I was signing the back of a million dollar check. I was beaming with excitement. Nathan looked right at me and said something

I thought I would never hear. He said, "You're free to go. Let me get the door for you." He swiped his key card and opened the door. "Take care Cindy. I hope I never see you back here."

As I walked through the door, I stopped to look back over my shoulder. I felt paranoid. I still felt like someone was going to reach out and grab me while I stepped out. My heart pounded through my chest. I continued on until I was outside of the hospital and free.

I couldn't believe it. I thought I was dreaming again. I was so happy to be out of that hell. The sun was shining, and the birds were going about their daily routines, chirping away at each other and flying from tree to tree. It was warm and cozy outside. I turned around and took one last look at the hospital building, raising my hand and putting up my middle finger. "Good riddance!" I said.

I was only minutes into my freedom when the thought of Anthony entered my mind. I need to find him. This is the first thing I need to do. I will let nothing or anyone get in my way of finding Anthony.

With no phone or way to get home, I stood here, trying to figure out what to do. First, I need to check the house for Anthony. How am I going to get there? I can't hitchhike. Nobody is going to pick up someone wearing scrubs and looking the way I do. Not to mention my hair. My hair is a mess and I still have staples in the back of my head. I feel like Frankenstein's monster and I'm not too far off from looking like him. Will there soon be a mob of village idiots chasing me down the street with pitchforks and torches? That seems to be my kind of luck these days. I feel like I'm living in a crazy horror novel, and this is just another page in my dysfunctional life.

I started walking to get as far away from this place as I could possibly get. Then it hit me, I could walk to the Feed and Grain store on the other side of town and ask Bill for a ride home. He will oblige my request for a ride. I'm sure he would love to hear all the insane tales about what I just went through.

I almost made it across town on foot when the sound of a car horn right behind me made me jump. As I looked back, I saw Vicky pulling up beside me. I tried to keep walking, but she kept on following me. I stopped, and she rolled down the window. "Cindy, get in. Please?"

I leaned down to look through the open window. "What do you want, Vicky?"

She had a sad look on her face. "I went to the hospital to see you so I could tell you I'm sorry. They said you were just released, so I've been driving around, trying to find you."

I rolled my eyes. "You still haven't answered my question, Vicky. What do you want?"

"Come on, Cindy, get in. Pretty please?"

As much as I hated her right now, I got in her car, anyway. I could use the ride. Besides, what would I do if Bill wasn't working today?

Vicky turned and looked at me, almost getting emotional. She said, "Listen, Cindy, I know you're upset with me and I'm sorry. Can you please forgive me? We've been best friends forever. I didn't mean to upset you."

"Fine, Vicky, but I'm going to need a little time to get over it. Just give me some space and don't hound me like you normally do," I said.

Her face brightened up. "That's all I ask of you. So, do you want a ride home? I can drop you off if you want me to? Please, I insist."

"Sure. I mean, I guess so."

"Okay, great. James is going to be so excited you are going home. I will call him now to let him know." She picked up her phone and called James. "Hey James, you're never going to guess who I have in the car with me? It's Cindy. Yes, they just released her. Are you at home? Great, I will bring her there. Okay, see you in an hour." She hung up the phone and said, "James is excited. He is going to be happy to see you."

I snarled, "Yeah, good for him."

We didn't talk about much on the ride. I didn't feel like talking. All I wanted to do was find Anthony. He is all I cared about. I'm sure the ride was just as awkward for Vicky. She drove much faster than she normally drives. Once we neared the house, Vicky pulled into the driveway and stopped to let me out.

"Here you are, Cindy. Enjoy your time at home. Call me soon."

She barely finished talking before I shut the car door on her. I needed to get inside and look for Anthony, so I rushed up the stairs and ran into the house.

I went down to Anthony's room, and he wasn't there. The bed appeared untouched, as if no one had slept in it. I checked the dresser drawers, and they were empty. I opened the closet door, and it was empty as well. It didn't look like he'd been staying here.

I need to go find James and ask him where Anthony went. He better not tell me he doesn't know who he is, either. As I turned toward the door to walk out, I noticed something underneath the bed. I got down on my knees and reached under. Oh, my gosh, it's one of Anthony's shirts. A soft button up flannel shirt. It must have gotten kicked under the bed and he forgot it there. I put the shirt up to my face and took a nice, long breath through my nose. It still smelled like him. I pressed it up against my face and snuggled right into it. I knew I wasn't crazy this whole time.

I pulled back the covers on the bed, leaned down and took in a big breath through my nose. The bed smells like Anthony too. I have to find James. He will know where Anthony is and I will make him tell me. What will he say about this shirt? How is he going to talk his way out of this one? I need to find James right now and confront him.

On my way to James's bedroom, I stopped in the kitchen and grabbed a small knife to put in my pocket. I don't trust him. I went and checked his bedroom. He wasn't there. His room smelled like a familiar perfume and his bed was messy. Not just one side of it like it usually is, but the entire bed. One pillow was pushed off to the side and the other pillow was lying on the floor next to the bed with red lipstick smudges on it. The blankets were pushed to the end, almost falling off, and the sheets were bunched up together. I glanced over to the bathroom and there were at least four towels strewn across the floor. This bastard has another woman in his bed while I'm locked away. I can't think about it right now. I need to focus and find Anthony.

I looked in every room for James but couldn't find him. He must be out back somewhere, I thought. I rushed out to the backyard and looked in the barn after not finding him in the yard. Still no James. Where the hell is he? I started calling for him and got no response.

I walked back to the house, opened the door and got startled when I saw James standing there looking at me with his hands in his pockets.

"Oh, hi Cindy. I was just on my way out to get you. I heard you calling for me."

"James, I checked the entire house, and you weren't in here. Where were you?"

He looked down the hall. "I was down in the basement. That's why you couldn't find me. I didn't expect you to be here so soon. I forgot how fast Vicky drives," he said.

I looked directly into his eyes as seriously as I could and said, "You and I need to talk. You might bullshit the doctors, but I know the truth. I'm not crazy, so tell me where the fuck Anthony is right now!"

"What the hell, Cindy! We have been over this too many times already. Get it through your head. There is no Anthony."

I raised Anthony's shirt and shook it in his face. "Then how do you explain this, James? This is one of Anthony's shirts he forgot under the bed. Here, take a good look at it."

He pulled his hands out of his pocket to grab the shirt from me.

"James, what the hell is that?"

He looked annoyed. "What now, Cindy?"

"Is that blood on your hands? Why do you have blood on your hands and why are your knuckles all beat up?"

James stood there with a blank expression on his face. I could tell he was getting annoyed and angry with me. He clenched his fists tight and started to open his mouth to speak. Then I heard a noise coming from the basement. It sounded like a raspy, wet cough followed by a painful moan.

I tried to make my way to the basement door, but James intentionally got in my way to block me. His eyes squinted below his menacing brows as he peered at me with contempt. His face was glowing red with anger. He tightened up his lips and with an assertive tone said, "If you know what's good for you, you won't go down there. I'm warning you, Cindy."

There is no way he is going to stop me from getting to the basement. That cough sounded like it came from Anthony. I shoved James hard, knocking him to the floor, and then ran to the door and down the steps into the basement.

The air in the basement is musty and stale. It's dim and dark with only two light bulbs lighting up the entire basement. There is no concrete slab for a floor, just dirt. The corners are filled with cobwebs left behind by spiders, and mouse droppings lined the floor along the walls.

I hated going into the basement. It creeped me out. It had the vibes of an old cemetery tomb or vault. It made my skin crawl. Whenever I came down here, I felt like there was something lurking in the dark, watching me, waiting to pounce on me to pull me back into the dark with it.

But today, the basement didn't scare me at all. A vicious demon from hell could pop out from nowhere and I would run right through it like a freight train to get to my Anthony. I glanced around to see if I could find him. I called out to him. "Anthony? Baby? Are you down here?"

Then I heard it again. A wet gurgling noise coming from the other side. Off in the distance, I could barely see a big pile of dirt that wasn't there before. I took off running toward the noise. As soon as I reached the other end, my world came crashing down by what I saw. I fell to my knees and screamed, "No!"

Anthony was on the ground with his arms behind him, hogtied with ropes, lying in front of a pit dug into the ground. His face was so bloodied and swollen, he was almost unrecognizable. There was blood running out of his nose and mouth. His eyes were so swollen shut, he couldn't see me even if he wanted to.

I placed my hand on his face. My eyes started welling up with tears. His skin felt hot to the touch and tacky from all the dried blood. "Anthony, baby? I'm here, it's Cindy. Please wake up," I said with a crackle in my voice. A tear fell from my eye and rolled down my cheek. I ripped my shirt off and placed it under his head. I couldn't believe what I was seeing. Anthony was just lying here, unconscious and almost lifeless. His breathing was shallow and labored. Blood gurgled from his mouth with every breath he took. I had to pull it together if I'm going to get him out of here and get him help. If I don't act quickly, he will die.

I reached over him to untie him without leaning on his battered body. I couldn't get the knots undone, and I kept struggling to free him. "Shit!" I said. Then I realized I grabbed a knife from the kitchen earlier, so I reached into my pocket and pulled out the knife. Again, I leaned over Anthony, carefully trying not to bump him or put any weight on him. Slowly, I started to slice through one of the ropes binding his hands together.

"Ow!" I screamed out in pain. The back of my head felt like someone was tearing through my skull. I accidentally dropped the knife down into the pit as my head was being pulled back. I realized someone had me by the hair and was yanking me back away from Anthony.

I heard James speak, "You can never mind your own fucking business and do what you're told, can you, Cindy?" James said as he kept on pulling my hair, making blood curdling screams come out of me. He pulled me up off of the ground, forcing me to stand there with my back to him.

"Cindy, you could have prevented this from happening, but you had to keep pushing. You just couldn't walk away from him. You forced my hand. It's all your fault, and now I have to be the one to get rid of him." James put his foot up onto Anthony and pushed him into the pit with one push of his leg. There was a big thud as Anthony hit the ground, accompanied by a loud snapping noise. I heard a whooshing gurgle and a soft groan come out of Anthony. I looked down into the dark pit and could faintly see a bone poking straight out of Anthony's arm.

"Stop it, James, you're going to kill him," I begged.

"That's the point of this whole thing, Cindy. I thought you were smarter than that?" James said, grinning at me.

I spun around and hit James in the face as hard as I could, hurting my hand. He stood there laughing at me. "Is that all you got?" Then he hit me with his open hand in the face, sending waves of pain throughout my injured head. I stood there, almost stumbling to the ground, spitting out some blood that was building up inside of my lip.

"Argh!" I screamed as I punched him right in the throat, causing him to choke. As he was holding his throat, I kneed him hard in the groin, making him bend over in pain. He started to stand straight up again. "Ugh! You're going to pay for that, bitch!" he screamed. Before I could react, he pulled his arm back and punched me in the face, knocking me down into the pit with Anthony. My fall almost crushed him. I got disoriented for a moment and could barely tolerate the pain radiating through my brain. Before I stood up, I grabbed the knife I dropped earlier, laying on the ground next to Anthony.

James stood at the edge of the pit. He was knee level to my face. "You don't give up easily, do you?" he asked.

"No, asshole, I don't." Then I plunged the knife deep into his thigh. He screamed out in pain and started hopping around. I tried to pull myself up and out of the hole I was standing in, but I couldn't get out. James noticed me struggling and limped back over to me. Before I could pull myself up, he kicked me in the face and sent me back down into the hole next to Anthony.

I blacked out for a minute. When I started to open my eyes, I could see James standing at the edge of the pit, looking down at me. His pants were soaked in blood where the knife was still stuck in his leg.

He reached behind his back and pulled his gun from his waistband, then pointed it at me. "Now I'm going to get rid of the two of you once and for all," he said. I put my hands up in front of my face. The last thing I heard was a loud bang and then darkness.

"James, no!" I screamed as I opened my eyes, still trembling with fear. Where am I? I looked around and realized I was on my bed and still in my room at the hospital. I ran over to the door and tried to open it. It was locked from the outside. I started beating on the door. "Let me out! Please, someone let me out!"

Nobody came. I was alone again and locked inside of my room. These nightmares have to stop at some point. I can't take them anymore. I'm afraid to go to sleep now. Am I in hell? It feels like I am. I don't know what reality is anymore. Is this what hell is really like? If it is, then I must be in hell. It's the only explanation

I can think of. Is this going to be my torment for eternity? I need to splash some cool water on my face to make sure I'm not still living in a nightmare. I turned to head toward the bathroom and there she was again, standing in the bathroom's doorway. "What are you doing here, Brenda? I thought I told you to leave and never come back? Get the hell out!" I yelled. She just stood there, staring at me. I screamed even louder. "Go!" Then she vanished.

I went into the bathroom and leaned over the sink. The cool water felt so good in my hands and even better on my face. I kept dousing my face in cold water until I was satisfied I was no longer living in a nightmare. I dried off with a towel and turned to walk out of the bathroom. There she was again, sitting on the side of my bed, staring at me and shaking her head in disgust.

"Brenda, I will not tell you again to leave me alone. I never want to see you again."

She stopped shaking her head just long enough to taunt me. "What are you going to do about it, bitch?" she said as she started to laugh at me. I could feel my blood start to boil. Anger took over me. I felt my face getting warm with rage. I ran out of the bathroom to jump on her and show her exactly what I was going to do about it.

As I charged through the doorway, my leg hit the corner of the dresser so hard it caused me to fall. As I fell, my head hit the bedpost, sending me to the floor with immense pain. There was a bright flash of light. A jolt of electricity tore through my head, setting my brain on fire. I wanted to scream out in pain but something miraculous happened. I remembered it all. A flashback from the day I got hurt played out in my mind. It was like my brain had been trying to tell me something. It just clicked and boom, I remembered what happened just like that. I know how I wound up here in the hospital and, more importantly, I know who it was that put me here.

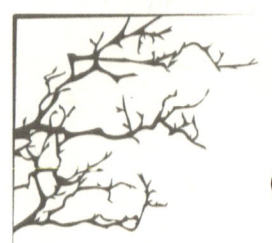

Chapter 24

It was late evening when James walked through the door from working all day. I just woke up from a nap and didn't know where Anthony was, so I was getting ready to go and find him. James looked at me with disgust. "What? No dinner again tonight, Cindy?"

"I'm so sorry, James. I figured you were going to be late, as always. I didn't make you a plate since you usually eat out before you come home. I can make you something real quick if you like?"

He got angry with me and said, "What are you good for anymore? What do you do all day while I'm at work busting my ass? Nothing?"

Did he really just say that to me? I don't know what his problem is, but I will not put up with it anymore. "Excuse me, James?" I said.

"You fucking heard me, Cindy. You are useless!"

I felt a rush of adrenaline flow through me and take over. "At least I haven't been having an affair our whole marriage, you spineless prick!"

He pointed his finger at me aggressively. The color in his eyes changed as he glared at me. "What did you say to me?"

I shouted back at him, "You heard me! I said you're a spineless prick!"

He clenched his jaw and made a fist. "I will show you who the spineless prick is!" He walked over to me, grabbed me by the throat, and pushed me up against the wall. "You better watch the way you speak to me or you will be sorry."

"You put your hand on me for the last time, asshole!" I lifted my knee, hitting him right in the groin. He let out a shrieking, painful scream. I tried to get away from him, but he grabbed my wrist and held on. "Let me go, you piece of shit," I yelled at him.

He stood up and grabbed me by the hair as I yelled out in pain. Then he pushed me onto the floor and he climbed on top of me, pinning me down. His weight almost suffocated me while he sat on me. I squirmed and tried to get free while he grabbed me by my hair, pulling my head up. Spit droplets were flying out of his mouth as he yelled, "You just don't know when to shut your fucking mouth, do you, bitch?" Then he lifted his arm and struck me across the face with his palm.

I screeched, "Ow, you bastard! Let me up so I can show you who the real bitch is!"

He tightened his grip on my hair. "Even now, you still can't keep your mouth shut!" Then he struck me again and dazed me good this time. My vision got blurry for a few seconds and I saw a flash of light when his hand contacted my face. The hit stung me and made my ears ring. My eyes started to water.

He stood up, looking down at me. That's when I kicked him as hard as I could in the groin again. This time he buckled over, holding his stomach while letting out a deep, painful groan. His face got very flush before he ran to the kitchen. I could hear him vomiting in the sink while I picked myself up off of the floor.

He was leaning up against the kitchen counter, taking deep breaths, when I went to confront him again. "James, I know all about your affair! You've been cheating on me for a long time! I'm going to divorce you and take you for everything you have! Do you hear me, you bastard?" I screamed, waving my finger in his face while he leaned up against the counter, trying to catch his breath from getting sick. "Marrying you was the biggest mistake of my life!"

He straightened his posture. "That is something we can both agree on! You aren't getting anything, you fucking bitch!"

I turned to walk away, and that's when James grabbed the cast-iron skillet from the stovetop. He swung it and struck me as hard as he could in the back of the head. Then I fell into darkness.

That's exactly what happened. It was James. He hit me in the head with the pan. He tried to kill me. That's why I'm in the hospital. It wasn't because of a horse riding accident. I was right all along. He wanted me dead, and he tried to kill me. I knew I wasn't crazy. All this time I had to put up with everyone thinking I was. What are they going to say when they find out James is the psychotic one?

For the first time, I couldn't wait for Dr. Lisa to come see me. I didn't want to keep this inside much longer. I felt like I was going to burst if I didn't get the truth out. I was ecstatic that my brain healed itself. The only piece of the puzzle that was left is how I got here. I remembered everything else except that, and now I know the truth. I can't wait to rub it in her face.

I am going to get out of this place and find Anthony so we can start our life together. I am going to get as far away from James as I can, and I hope he goes to prison for what he did to me. And speaking of prison, once the police know the truth about what happened, James will spend the rest of his life there. I can't wait to see that asshole rot behind bars for what he did to me, if he lasts that long. Everyone knows what happens to guys that go to prison for hurting women. I just hope they make him suffer before they kill him.

And Vicky, I can't wait to throw it in her face too. She turned her back on me when I needed her the most and betrayed me. She has now lost a close friend because I will never trust her again. I don't need people like her in my life. As a matter of fact, I only need one person in my life to make me happy, and that is Anthony.

The next morning, I was excited to see Dr. Lisa's face through the small window in my door. It felt like I had to wait forever. It was the first time I was happy to have her come into my room so I can tell her the truth about what happened to me. This time, I wanted to talk. I hope she calls the police right away so I can fill out a report and tell them what James did to me. Too bad I won't be there to see the look on his face when they slap the cuffs on him for attempted murder. I guess I will get some satisfaction when I'm in court testifying about his crime.

The first thing I'm going to do when I get out of here is divorce him, get my house, and make him pay for what he's done. I will write to him in prison just to let him know how happy I am raising a family with Anthony in the home he bought.

Dr. Lisa walked into my room with a couple of hospital security guards again. I don't blame her. I attacked her and threatened to kill her. The sight of the guards didn't bother me. The news I have for her is too exciting to bring me down today. She stood beside the guards, almost behind them. As calm as Dr.

Lisa always is, I could tell something was troubling her. "Cindy, we need to talk, and I need you to stay calm or the guards will put you in restraints." She pointed at one of the guards holding what looked like leather cuffs and straps. "James is here, and he has some paperwork for you. I can explain it to you if you want him to leave and I will understand if you don't want to see him," she said, looking out into the hall.

"No, it's fine. I want to see the look on his face when I confront him with the truth. I'm sure it's divorce papers and I will happily sign them."

"Cindy, I have spoken with James and he knows if you ask him to leave, he is to leave right away," she assured me.

"Okay, fine Lisa."

Dr. Lisa stepped out into the hall to get James. They came back together a minute later. James had some papers in his hand. He stood there staring at me for a minute. The look on his face was evil and sinister. I could tell that he was up to something and I didn't like it.

"What do you want, James? I'm not in the mood for your bullshit," I said, staring back at him.

He started to speak. "Cindy, I just need you to hear me out, as I have your best interest at heart and I think you need help. I care about you and feel you have backed me into a corner. I've been telling you for a while that you should get help and my requests just go on, ignored by you. You have left me no choice."

"Just spit it out, James. I'm not in the mood for any of your games today."

He moved closer to me and reached out his arm to hand me some paperwork. I grabbed it while he stepped back next to the hospital guards and read what he just gave me. "These are court papers? An Emergency Order for Involuntary Commitment? What is this, James?"

"It's for the best Cindy. It's ordering you to get some help before you can come home."

I read on in disbelief. "This paper says I am to be remanded to the state psychiatric hospital until I'm deemed safe, pending treatment and evaluation until further notice of the court. How is this possible? What did you do to me, James?"

"I'm sorry, Cindy, but I petitioned the court to order you to get treatment. I have too many concerns about your behavior and so doesn't Dr. Lisa. She wrote a recommendation to the court so we can get you the help you need."

"Until I am deemed safe? You bastard! Why don't you tell the doctor who the actual monster is, James? You're the one who needs to be locked up in a mental ward! I know what you did to me. Why don't you tell the doctor how I got here! Go ahead, tell her, you psycho! Tell her how you smashed me in the back of the head to kill me so you and your lover could get rid of me. Anthony told me all about it. I remember what you did to me. I'm going to have you arrested!"

"Cindy, this is what I'm talking about! I don't know who the hell Anthony is and now you're accusing me of trying to kill you? You're sick! That's why I had to do what I did. Something is seriously wrong with you!"

I looked right at Dr. Lisa. "You, of all people! I confided in you and this is how you treat me? You help this monster lock me up? I will kill the both of you for doing this to me!" I couldn't contain myself any longer. I didn't know what I did to deserve this. It's not fair. I started crying and throwing anything I could get my hands on at the both of them. I tried to stand up and catch them as they ran out of my room, but my legs were shaking violently and the guards got in my way.

"Both of you will get what's coming to you. I promise this isn't the last you will see of me! You will be sorry you ever met me, James!" It was only seconds before three or four of the staff came running in to help the guards hold me down. I felt a sharp sting and minutes later, I was asleep.

I woke to the feeling of someone shaking my leg. I opened my eyes, still in a daze, to see Dr. Lisa standing at the foot of my bed. Immediately, I looked around to see if anyone else was in the room with her and there was no one.

"What do you want, you backstabber?" I muttered.

"I am here to talk to you about why I think it's best that you get treatment and what that is going to look like for you. There is no need to get up or have another episode of aggression. You are in restraints."

I tried to pick up my arm to see if she was telling the truth and I couldn't get up because my wrists were cuffed with straps that were tied to the bed. My ankles suffered the same fate as my wrists. I snarled at Dr. Lisa. "You know when I get out of here I am going to find James and take care of him myself?"

"Cindy, that is one reason we feel it is necessary to get you help. You are a risk to the safety of others and maybe yourself at this point. I've been doing this for a very long time, and I am concerned about your behavior and threats."

"I'm a risk? Have you evaluated the psycho I married? There is nothing wrong with me. It's James you should be concerned with."

"Cindy, I know that this is very difficult for you to hear, but you need to hear it and understand it so you can attempt to get better. There are a multitude of reasons I am doing this. You're showing signs of Paranoid Schizophrenia. You have delusions and hallucinations that just aren't true, believing in a person who doesn't exist. You also suffer from episodes of Akinetic Catatonia. You stare out into nothing, while you're in a stupor, grimacing. You have an obsessive love disorder with an imaginary person. The aggression and threats against your husband's life are all very serious and you need treatment to get your life back before someone gets seriously hurt."

"I don't understand, Dr. Lisa. Why are you doing this to me? Anthony is real. He is a real person! Why don't you believe me? James is the liar! He is trying to get rid of me. That's why I am here. He tried to kill me and he is going to kill Anthony if you don't let me out of here. You have to believe me!" I started sobbing. I felt trapped again with the realization that I was on my own and there was nothing I could do about it.

"Cindy, I know this is difficult, but we are going to get you the help you need."

"You don't know shit, Lisa! If you knew anything, I wouldn't be here and you wouldn't be locking up the wrong person! The real threat is James, not me! You need to believe me. He is going to end up seriously hurting someone, starting with Anthony. You need to call the cops so they can protect him. Please, I'm begging you."

Dr. Lisa just stood there, not paying any mind to what I was saying. My words were going in one ear and out the other. Ugh, I just want to reach out and strangle her to death.

"Cindy, once the doctor clears you for transport, they will move you to the State Psychiatric Hospital that's not very far from here. I wish you the best of luck and I sincerely mean that. It was a pleasure getting to know you."

"Yup! I wish I could say the same about you, Lisa. I hope I never see your face again."

Dr. Lisa walked out of the room and I cried myself to sleep.

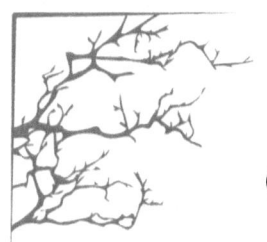

Chapter 25

I'm not sure how many days went by before they moved me to the other hospital. I have been in a trance-like state ever since my last visit with the back stabbing shrink. They came in, strapped me into a wheelchair with restraints and loaded me into a van.

The drive to the other hospital didn't take long. I was surprised when I saw the building. I have passed it a couple of times on my way around town, but never quite knew what it was. There was no locked gate we had to drive through. No security guards hanging around. No big sign saying stay out because of the mentally ill. Just an enormous brick building. I'm sure anyone who sees this place doesn't even know it houses the mentally insane. I thought the lack of security seemed strange until I saw the person who was bringing me into the building using a key card to get access. I soon realized that most areas of the hospital required a key card. Without one, there is no getting in or out of this place.

The intake process was like something out of a prison movie other than the blood pressure and health check. They made me strip down so the nurse could check me for contraband or anything that could harm me or somebody else. They gave me a standard pair of white hospital scrubs with the hospital name written across the back to differentiate the patients from the staff.

This place gives me the creeps. Everything is white, from the floors to the ceilings. It has that distinct hospital smell. Big, locked double doors separated each area. There isn't much to the place. There is a cafeteria, a few halls that housed the bedrooms, a locked staff area where patients couldn't go, and a room that they called the "common area." The common area is where patients go to spend their days playing games at the tables, watching t.v. or just talking to one another to pass the time.

My room is empty except for a metal, bench style bed that was attached to the wall and a stainless steel toilet. The bed had a mattress with no sheet and a pillow with no pillow case on it. The walls and ceiling were a bright white paint and there was a long light in the ceiling that was too high to reach. One wall has a small window with bars on it. It is high up and unreachable, just like the ceiling light. Its only purpose was to let daylight in, I assume. The door to the room was a heavy metal door that can get locked on the outside. It had a small window, with bars, for the staff to look through when the door was closed. I assume my bedroom was like an empty cell because they think I might be a safety risk to myself.

After my intake, they brought me to the common area, but all I wanted to do was curl up on my bed and cry myself to sleep. Everybody was sitting in chairs doing nothing. One lady was talking to herself nonstop, others were staring out the windows, and some were sleeping in their chairs while sitting up. There was this one guy sitting by himself in the corner who was annoying. Every time I would look in his direction, he would point at me and start laughing out loud. He made me feel very uneasy, so I made it a point to not look at him.

I could tell that everybody has been here a long time just by looking at their complexion. They are all very pale and have had no direct sunlight in quite some time. Everyone also seemed very drugged and out of it. Do they even let people outside at all? It doesn't seem like it.

This must be the part of the hospital where they keep only the extremely ill patients. I don't understand why this is where they would place me? I'm not crazy and even if I was just a little insane, I don't feel like I belong in a place with people as crazy as this. These patients are out of it. I feel like after enough time in a place like this, even the sane could become insane.

My daily routine was very mundane and boring. Wake up, eat breakfast, get medication, watch t.v., eat lunch, get medication, watch t.v., eat dinner, watch t.v. and then go to bed. Sleeping during the day after crying myself to sleep was the only thing that broke up my routine.

I still thought about Brenda occasionally. Sometimes, while I lay in bed, I could still see her standing outside of my door, staring in at me with a grimace on her face. It was as if she wanted to torment me or remind me she will never permanently go away for good. I'm going to have to accept seeing her from time to time throughout my life. If I think about it, it's really not so bad. She has been in my life forever and I'm used to her being around.

After about a week, I started getting sick. I had to keep rushing to the bathroom to vomit. It must be the disgusting food they serve here or the bullshit medications they have me on. I will not last here much longer, so I need to get out and find Anthony. If there was only a way I could get a hold of one of the keycards that all the nurses carry around their necks on a lanyard, I could get out of here.

James came by twice since I got admitted. The first time it was to visit me and see how I was doing. It didn't go over well. I flipped out and caused a scene because he was here. The second time, I saw him walk past my door to go meet with the doctor. I assume it was to get an update on my condition. I honestly don't understand why he would even care. If you ask me, I bet he's here to get an assurance from the doctor that I'm never getting out of here.

Seeing James elevated my emotions. The hate and disdain I have for him just keeps growing the more I see him or think about him. I never in my life thought that I would ever wish anyone dead, but I want him dead, even if it has to be by my hands. I'm okay with killing James now. After what he put me through and how he was getting away with attempted murder, it would be easy for me to kill him now. After all, he tried to kill me. It's not my fault he didn't succeed in doing so. Maybe someday I will get my revenge on him and have the chance to snuff out his life for good.

The following week went by faster than usual. I learned that if I freak out and try to attack the staff, they would drug me and restrain me in a chair long enough for the medication to kick in. Once I calmed down, they would let me out of the chair so I could lie in my bed and sleep. Sleeping was the only thing I wanted to do to pass the time. I couldn't handle the reality of being locked up in a place like this, not to mention I had to start my therapy sessions this week.

My therapy sessions didn't go well. After trusting Dr. Lisa and having it backfire on me, I refused to talk to this doctor, which is what I should have done from the start with Dr. Lisa. If I would have just kept my stupid mouth shut, I wouldn't be here. I never should have told her anything. I'm learning there are only two people in this world I can trust, myself and Anthony.

So, that's what I do with this doctor. I sit here and ignore him. I act like he isn't even here. It annoys him, but I don't care. Who do these doctors think they are? They think they can just lock someone up against their will while they live a life of freedom? Do they even think about us when they are at home with their families? I bet they don't. Pricks.

I couldn't stop thinking about Anthony. Thoughts of him consumed my brain like nothing else. It was a vicious cycle. I would think of him and then I would cry. This would happen over and over every day. It won't be long before I am crazy and sitting with the mindless patients in the common area. There has to be a way out of here. I can't stay here. I need to get out. But how? This place is locked down pretty good. The only way in and out of here are the key cards hanging from the necks of the workers and staff.

I was sitting in a gurney style chair. It was one of the mobile chairs the staff moves you around in. A chair on wheels with restraints for unruly patients, such as myself. I had straps holding my legs at the ankles, straps securing my arms and wrists and a strap that went around my body. They secured me to the chair because I started screaming, throwing things and threatening the orderlies. They also jabbed me with a needle and injected something to calm me down. The medication has already kicked in. I felt calm and everything was hazy. It felt good. I felt numb to the emotional pain I was going through.

Once I had my "episode" as they call it, two of the staff grabbed me, shoved me into the chair and held me there while another person strapped me in. Once they administered a shot to my shoulder, they wheeled me down the hall and into my room, where they left me.

I sat there, strapped to the chair, in the middle of the room, facing the open door. The only thing I could see was the empty hall and a closed door across the hall. It matched the door of the room I was in. I would see the nurses glance at me as they walked by.

I closed my eyes for a couple of minutes to escape the hell I was in. I would drift off and daydream about Anthony, longing for the day I walk out of this place and right into his arms. I'm imagining what it's going to be like living together, without James. I can't wait to get out and divorce my asshole husband so I can marry the man of my dreams.

I opened my eyes to the sound of footsteps entering the room. I assumed it was the nurse coming to let me out of my chair and to tell me to go to bed, now that the drugs have taken effect.

"Oh, shit!" I said, startled by who I saw standing in front of me.

"What... what the hell are you doing here, James?"

"Well, well, well. You're where you belong, Cindy, and you're alive, unfortunately. I just wanted to come by and see you one last time. Oh, and to tell you something."

"What the hell do you want, asshole?" I said, wishing I could reach out my arms and strangle him to death.

"Cindy, I just wanted to tell you that you are right."

"What? I'm confused," I said.

"After a head injury like that, who wouldn't be confused? So I'm going to spell it out for you real slow. You're right, I lied. You're not crazy."

"James, what did you lie about?"

"First, let's start with why I was never home and always on my so-called 'work trips'. Or why I have always turned down your pitiful sexual advances towards me. I've been cheating on you ever since we got married. And with whom, you might ask? Oh, you're going to love this, Cindy. I've been cheating on you with Vicky ever since we were in college. That's right, I've been seeing your best friend behind your back all along. I'm in love with her. I would have married her after college, but she didn't want to be tied down then. So I settled for you. That was a big mistake. It's okay though, she changed her mind and we will tie the knot soon."

"You bastard, James! I should have killed you when I had the chance."

"That's too bad, Cindy. At least one of us had the balls to follow through. The night I crushed your head in with a pan, I thought I got rid of you for good. I even carried you out to the field and laid your head down on a rock, where I left you for a few hours to make sure you were dead before I called the authorities. I told them I found you like that when I got home. All I had to do was saddle up a horse and let it loose in the field with you. Yet, here you are, still alive."

I looked James in the face and said, "When I get out of here, I am going to finish what I started."

"Don't worry, Cindy. I'm going to make sure that you never get out. It must be tough to rot in here every day, missing your little lover boy, Anthony. I know all about you and your love affair. Vicky rushed right over to me and told me all about it the day you confided in her. I had to see it for myself, so I followed the two of you on the weekend you thought I was away. The look on your face when you saw me in the parking lot that day was priceless. You looked like you saw a ghost."

"I warned your boyfriend, once already, that he better not touch my wife. Now either of us has to worry about him. You're never going to see your precious little Anthony again. Do you want to know why, Cindy?"

James grabbed me by my hair, snapped my head back, leaned down and whispered something into my ear that enraged me. I snapped and started screaming as he walked out of the room, laughing. "I'm going to fucking kill you, James! Do you hear me? You're dead to me! You are fucking dead!"

Two nurses came running in to see what the problem was.

"Calm down, Cindy. Just calm down."

"No, I will not calm down! I told you I wasn't crazy. I was right all along and I wasn't lying. James was the one lying. He tried to kill me. It wasn't an accident. He just confessed everything to me. He was just here."

"Who was here?" the nurse asked.

"James! He was just in here. He told me everything."

"Cindy, calm down. You're having another episode. Nobody was here. It's all in your mind. I know it seems very real to you, but I assure you it's not. That's why you're here, sweetie. So you can get some help."

I started to cry.

"Listen, Cindy. It's going to be bedtime soon. Can you promise me you will calm down? Then I will come back and get you out of this chair so you can get a good night's sleep. I think you just need to get some good rest. You haven't been sleeping that well."

Here I sat, thinking that there was no way I'm this crazy. I know what I have to do. I have to get out of here so I can kill James and find Anthony. That's the only way I can be with Anthony again.

It wasn't long before the nurse came back to unstrap me from the chair. As soon as she got the last strap off, I grabbed her by the head and sunk my teeth right into the side of her face as deep as they would go. She let out a loud shriek, so I slammed her head into the wall. She fell to the floor, out cold.

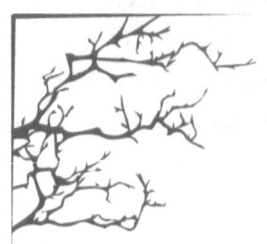

Chapter 26

I found myself standing over James one last time. Only this time I wasn't standing here nude. I was still in my hospital scrubs. And this time, I wasn't holding a knife. It was his hunting rifle I was holding. I had no sense of what time it was. I just knew that it was dark outside.

James was sleeping on his side, close to the edge of the bed, facing my direction.

"Wake up, James," I said as I poked him in the face with the end of the rifle barrel.

He opened his eyes to see me standing there with a gun pointed at him. He jumped. "Oh shit! Cindy, what are you doing here? Why do you have a gun? Oh my God, did you escape from the hospital?"

"Shut your mouth or I will shoot you right here! You and I are going to take a little walk together."

"Walk... where?" he stuttered, trembling with fear.

"Get up, James. Get the fuck up!"

He crawled off of the bed and stood up while I kept the rifle pointed at him. "We're going to the barn, James. Start walking and don't say a word to me or I will shoot you," I told him, while keeping the rifle up against his back. We made our way to the barn and walked in. It was dim inside with only a few light bulbs lighting up the whole barn. I placed the rifle up against the wall and grabbed the knife we cut the hay bale strings with from the workbench.

"The stall over there without the horse. Get in there," I said while pointing the knife toward the stall. He walked over while I pushed him along. "Get the fuck in there!" I yelled as I pushed him into the stall. He stumbled and fell to the floor.

"James, you need to help me. Please James. Please help me."

"Shut the fuck up, Vicky!" I screamed.

James lifted his head and looked at her. "Oh, my God, Cindy, why is Vicky tied to the wall naked?"

"I wanted you and your whore to be together, James."

Before I brought James out, I forced Vicky up against the wall, stretched out her arms and bound her to the boards. Then I took it upon myself to terrorize her by methodically cutting all her clothes off.

"James, isn't she so pretty, even with the belly she's getting?" I walked out to the flowers I placed on the table for Anthony and grabbed one of the daisies. "Vicky, did you know daisies are the most common flowers placed at graves?" I asked her, while placing the flower in her hair.

Vicky started crying and pleading with me. "Please Cindy, I'm begging you, please let me go."

"Shut up, skank, or I will cut you." She started crying harder and sobbing. I got a lot of joy out of watching her cry. It excited me. I almost wanted to stand there and count the tears running down her face and make her cry even harder.

"Get up, James, and stand up against the wall, right next to this whore." He got up and moved over to the wall at a crawling pace while I kept the knife pointed at him.

"Back up to the wall and stretch out your arms!" I said.

He begged me, "You don't have to do this, Cindy. Just let us go. We won't tell anyone about this."

"Yes, please, Cindy," Vicky said, while still sobbing.

"If I hear another word out of either of you, I will cut your throats right here!"

I tied James's wrists to the boards, and I enjoyed the scared, terrified look on his face, but it wasn't enough for me. I wanted more. I needed to humiliate him and watch him suffer. I wanted to see his pain, and I wanted to hear him begging for his life. I put the tip of the knife up to his throat and held it there for a few seconds while he took a big gulp. He started to tremble and shake. "Don't shake too much, James, I just might accidentally cut you." I said, while laughing. Then, just as I did to Vicky, I slowly cut his shirt off while basking in pleasure at his torment. As soon as I finished, I pulled his pajama pants and boxers down around his ankles.

"Kick them off, James." He pulled one foot out, and with the other, he kicked his clothes across the stall.

"Be a good boy, James, or I just might cut off your little dick and shove it into your girlfriend's mouth to keep her quiet. Now, let me get a good look at the two of you."

I took a few steps back to take a nice long look at what I've accomplished so far and I was so proud of myself. I couldn't help but smile. It made me so happy to watch them tremble with fear. I found great pleasure in their suffering.

I walked over to Vicky. She started squirming as I approached her. "You! Of all people. You were my best friend. James told me all about the two of you. You can't ever keep your hands to yourself. No, Vicky has to have it all. First, you sleep with my husband and then you try to take Anthony from me. You will not get away with this, Vicky! You're going to pay for what you did."

"Cindy, please. Whatever James told you, he is lying."

"Vicky, I don't know what she is talking about."

"Shut the fuck up, James! Or I will cut your little girlfriend right here in front of you." I reached up, grabbed her by the hair, and put the knife to her throat. "You better tell me where Anthony is, Vicky!"

"I don't know who Anthony is. Cindy, please. I don't know what you're talking about."

"Bitch, you do know what I'm talking about! I told you all about him when you came by to see me. You wanted to borrow him for a night. Now you don't remember because this piece of shit is standing next to you? You're a fucking liar!" I screamed.

"Cindy, you're not well. Please, just let us go. You need help. Let us help you. You need to go back to the hospital," she said.

I stood there, staring right through her. My head started ringing harder and hurting more and more. I put my hands on my head and screamed, "Ah!" I then turned my attention to James.

"You better tell me where Anthony is, James!"

"I don't know who Anthony is."

"Yes, you do! You hired him and he stayed with us. He built the planter box sitting in our backyard! What did you do to him, James? Did you kill him like you said you would? Did you fucking kill him?"

"Cindy, that planter box was here when we moved in. Don't you remember? There is no Anthony. It's all in your head. You're not well. Please let us take you back to the hospital. I would never kill anyone and I would never cheat on you. You're my wife. I love you, baby."

"Don't you call me baby! That is what Anthony calls me, you piece of shit!"

I stepped back in front of Vicky and raised the knife. She started sobbing and begging me not to hurt her. I cut the rope that was binding her hands, grabbed her by the hair and said, "Let's go, bitch." I started dragging her out of the barn. I could hear James screaming and asking me where I was taking her. He was begging me to stop. Once I was done with Vicky, I went back into the barn for James. I picked up the rifle, went into the stall, and cut him free.

"Where is Vicky? What did you do with her?"

"Walk, James." I walked him out of the barn and over to the planter box that my love built for me.

"Oh, fuck. Oh, shit. You killed her? You really killed her? Why are you doing this, Cindy?" He started sobbing and begging me to stop as he looked down at her lifeless body laying in the box. There was a pool of blood under her head and torso. He could see the knife wound in her throat. She wasn't moving, and her eyes were stuck open.

"James, you should have heard her begging for her life. It was so sweet and moving. I wanted to feel bad, but I didn't. Now get in the box. Lay down beside your girlfriend."

"Don't do this Cindy. Please, I'm begging you."

I picked up the rifle and hit him in the face with it. He fell, tripping over the side, landing on top of Vicky. He moved off of her in a flash, looked up at me, and kept pleading for his life.

I pointed the gun right at his face and said, "Now you and Vicky can be together forever. Isn't that so sweet, James?" I squeezed the trigger, and he fell limp. I stood there, staring at both of them while smiling. Then I thought about what my sweet love Anthony said about filling the box. I took one last look at their lifeless bodies and thought to myself, fertilizer, and laughed out loud. I threw the rifle into the box with them and went back to the barn.

I placed the bloody knife back on the workbench and started calling out for my love. "Anthony, where are you? Baby, I'm home and I need you. Please, baby, come to me."

I sat down on the floor and leaned up against the wall. I brought my knees up, tucked my face into my legs, and began to cry. That's right where the sheriff found me in the early morning.

"Cindy, are you okay? They told me you attacked a nurse and snuck out of the hospital. I thought I might find you here. Why do you have blood on your hand?" He glanced around and spotted the bloody knife on the workbench. "Are you hurt or did you hurt someone?"

I knew it was Ethan by the sound of his voice, so I picked up my head and began to cry. I looked right at him and said, "I don't know." My brain was foggy, and the ringing in my head wouldn't go away.

"Come on, let's get you up and get you back to the hospital so we can figure out what's going on. You shouldn't be here." He helped me get up, and as he did, I grabbed the shovel near me that was leaning up against the wall. I took a hard swing and hit him on the side of the head. He stumbled, falling to the ground, and rolling onto his back. I swung at him again and he put up his arms to protect his head. The shovel hit his arm, and he screamed out in pain. I stood over him and raised the shovel high over my head, and got ready to hit him with everything I had, just to put an end to this.

"I want to know where Anthony is! Where... the fuck... is Anthony?" I screamed at him. I heard a loud bang and saw a flash of light. The searing, burning pain in my chest caused me to topple over and fall to the ground. Then... darkness.

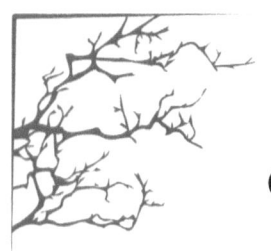

Chapter 27

"Hey, Sheriff."

"Hey, Doc, how is she doing? Any updates?"

"Well, she has made a full recovery from the gunshot wound to her chest, but psychologically, she's not doing any better. As a matter of fact, she is getting worse as time goes on. We have to keep her pretty sedated and have her in restraints most of the time, or she tries to attack the staff violently. Her delusions are becoming more frequent and her hallucinations are intensifying. She spends much of her time staring out into nothing and crying out for Anthony. Have you been able to find out anything about this guy?"

"No, nothing at all. We looked for him and checked with people who knew Cindy, places and stores that she frequented, and nobody ever saw her with anyone. If he exists, it's in her head. A figment of her imagination."

"So Sheriff, how many people did she kill?"

"Just the husband. She attempted to murder her best friend Vicky and almost succeeded. She had a pretty bad knife wound to the throat and lost a lot of blood, but by some miracle survived. She barely had a pulse when we found her. I guess she and the husband were having an affair, and she was pregnant with the husband's baby. Vicky ended up losing the baby from all the blood loss. The husband and girlfriend were both found lying naked together when we found them, which raised a lot of questions and led us to believe that Cindy was aware of what was going on between the two of them. She must have found out about it and snapped."

"Speaking of pregnancy, Sheriff, I hate to be the bearer of bad news, but there is one more complication."

"Complication? How can things get any worse?"

"Well, Sheriff, it just so happens that Cindy is also pregnant."

"What! How far along is she?"

"Not far at all. It must have happened right before her injury, which is why the hospital didn't pick up on it. We tested her when she started getting sick and not feeling well. To be honest, I'm surprised that after everything she has been through, she hasn't had a miscarriage by now."

"That's a real shame, doctor. That child is going to be thrown right into foster care without a mom or dad. I do not want to be around when they take the baby from her. All hell is going to break loose. It breaks my heart."

"What was the court's ruling? If you don't mind me asking, Sheriff."

"The judge decided she is not fit to stand trial, and she's mentally incompetent, so she will serve out her life sentence here at the Maximum Security Psychiatric Unit. You should have the court order sometime this week."

"I will give my staff a heads up. We were kind of expecting her to be placed here permanently. It's a real shame when this stuff happens. It's heartbreaking to have to watch Cindy and people like her suffer with these illnesses."

The Sheriff looked through the door window. Strapped into a chair with her head down, sat Cindy. She had a small puddle of drool on her lap that had been running out of her mouth. She then raised her head in a slow manner and gave the Sheriff an evil blank stare and grimacing smile. He jumped back from the door, startled.

"Doc, I hate to say this, but I don't recognize her anymore. Cindy is no longer there. I don't know what kind of monster has taken her over, I just know one thing for sure... that's not Cindy. Here's my direct number. If there are any changes in her condition, please call me and let me know."

"Sure thing, Sheriff. You will be the first to know."

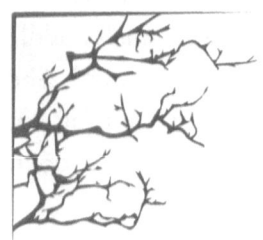

Chapter 28

"Daddy."

"Yes, Willow?"

"Where are we? This place looks creepy. It looks run down and abandoned."

"Yeah, no one has lived here in some time."

"So why are we here?"

"I just wanted to see it one last time."

"You've been here before?"

"Yes, sweetheart. A long time ago, I worked for a very special woman who lived here. I loved her very much. Her name was Cindy."

"That's mommy's name. I wish I knew her. It's not fair she died giving birth to me."

"Come on, Willow, take a walk with me. I want to show you the beautiful tree you got your name from, and I will tell you all about your mom."

"Daddy, one day I want to be just like mommy."

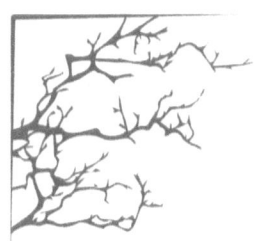

Chapter 29

It has been ten years since Cindy attempted to take my life by cutting my throat, killed my baby, and murdered my lover, James. After Cindy's death and a paternity test, Anthony took custody of his daughter Willow and moved back into the farmhouse after purchasing it from the bank. Now that Anthony is dead and out of the picture for good, there is only one more person I need to take care of. Once enough time passes and things blow over, she will suffer the same fate. As my favorite saying goes, "If there is serious injury, you are to take life for life, eye for eye, tooth for tooth." I will take what has been taken from me and I will have great pleasure in doing so.

"Hello, Vicky. Congratulations, the adoption went through. I assume you are here to pick her up?"

"Yes, how is she doing?"

"She seems to be doing better, but she is still suffering from some trauma. I can't even imagine how horrifying it is for her to lose both parents. No child should have to go through what Willow had to endure. It's heartbreaking when parents leave behind a young child. First, her mom gets locked away for life and then her dad ends up disappearing. It's so sad."

"I agree, wholeheartedly," I said.

"Vicky, I just want to say you are so brave to be adopting her after what her mother did to you. I really mean it. I'm sure it hasn't been easy for you to make a decision like this. Anyway, Willow is in the room over there. I will go get her and bring her out to you. I bet she is going to be excited to be going back home."

When she brought Willow out to me, the room started to spin, and I felt like I was going to pass out. Once I saw her, I couldn't help but see Cindy's face smiling and laughing at me while I pleaded for my life, right before she cut my throat and left me for dead. It was almost as if I was looking at Cindy herself. The resemblance to her mother is striking. Willow's blonde wavy hair, bright sparkling blue eyes and facial features made me feel like her mother was back from the dead. She looks so much like Cindy. It's going to be a struggle for me to look at her every day. I need to remind myself it's only temporary until I bury her with her parents.

"Here she is, Vicky. Are you okay? You look a little flush."

"Yes, I'm fine. I'm just a little emotional. Hi, Willow, I'm Vicky. I knew your mom. I'm going to be taking care of you from now on. Are you ready to go home?"

She stood there, looking through me with no emotion or expression on her face, saying nothing. I asked again, "Willow? Are you ready to go home?"

"She is a little shy, Vicky. Once she gets to know you, I'm sure she will warm up to you."

"You're probably right. I'm sure she'll be fine," I said.

The car ride to the house didn't go much better than our introduction. Willow sat in the passenger seat next to me and didn't say a word the entire ride. She just stared out the window, never looking in my direction. There is something strange about her that makes me feel uneasy. I'm not sure what it is, but something about her is off and it makes me not trust her, regardless of the fact she is only a child.

As soon as I turned into the driveway and saw the house, I almost started to panic and turn back around. I have visited the farm only once since that horrific night, but being here today with Willow made it feel eerie. It scared me. Once I saw the barn, I had to look away.

Willow knew something was wrong. I was visibly shaken. She turned toward me and finally spoke. "Are you alright, Vicky?"

"Yes, I'm okay. I don't like the barn. It creeps me out."

"I understand. It creeps me out, too," she said.

"Willow, you can call me auntie. It sounds so much better than Vicky."

"Okay, Auntie Vicky," she said while jumping out of the car and running for the door.

As soon as we walked into the house, Willow went down to her room and shut the door behind her. Looking around the place brought back memories I didn't want to think about. I remember the night Cindy tried to take my life all too well, like it was yesterday.

James and I were asleep in bed and I woke up thirsty, so I went to the kitchen to get a glass of water. It was really dark and I could barely see as I made my way across the house. Once I neared the kitchen, what looked like a dark figure standing in the hall startled me. I jumped and almost took off running back toward James's bedroom.

"Come on, you're being ridiculous," I said. There is no way someone is in here, I thought. I walked back toward the hall next to the kitchen, taking slow steps and being as quiet as I could be. I reached out and flipped the light switch on. I let out a sigh of relief when I saw no one standing there. "You're being paranoid. You need to calm down," I told myself. I went to the cabinet to get a glass, and that's when a hand reached around me from behind and covered my mouth. I almost passed out as I stood there frozen and trembling in fear.

"Hello, Vicky. Are you enjoying your night in James's bed?" I heard Cindy say. I tried to scream, but couldn't. Then I felt the cold, sharp blade of a knife press up against my throat.

"You and I are going to take a little walk and if I were you, I wouldn't make a sound," she said. A tear drop ran out from the corner of my eye and down my cheek as she walked me out to the barn. I could barely walk or feel my legs from the fear that overcame me. Why is she bringing me to the barn and what does she plan on doing with me? I tried pleading with her, but she would only tell me to shut up and then threaten to kill me.

I will forever remember the night when Cindy smiled and laughed in my face while she cut into my throat. Not a day goes by where it doesn't cross my mind. I just wish Cindy was here so I could return the favor and make her pay for all she had done to me. Although, I now have her daughter Willow, and she will do just fine in fulfilling her mother's debt to me. It's now only a matter of time before she will.

Willow spent the rest of the day in her room. She didn't come out to eat or use the bathroom once. I'm not sure what she did in there all day? At bedtime, when I went and tucked her into bed, she never said a word to me. She just laid down, pulled the blankets up, and went to sleep. Such a strange girl, I thought.

Once she was asleep, I wandered through the house looking around. The guest room where Anthony slept is still a little messy. The drawers and closet are still full of his clothes and belongings. I'm sure he continued to sleep in this room because it's where he and Cindy slept. I assume he never got over Cindy's death.

I made my way down to James's bedroom, where we spent many nights together. When I opened the door, I was shocked by what I saw. Everything is covered with a light layer of dust. Clothes and towels are scattered on the floor, and the bed remains a mess, as if nobody has touched it since that horrific night when Cindy executed James and attempted to kill me. Anthony must have his reasons for not wanting to come into this room, and it showed.

I opened one of the dresser drawers and saw folded tee shirts, neatly stacked. They belong to James. I pulled one out and smelled it. I miss him so much. I laid on the bed and curled up. I pulled his pillow close to me and snuggled into it. How can Cindy be so evil? I should have married James after college. It's all my fault. If I would have married him when he wanted to marry me, none of this would have ever happened and James would still be here, alive. I don't know how I'm going to continue on without him. I think about him and our baby every day and it never gets any easier.

I became emotional and felt my eyes fill with tears. I can't sleep in here. I'm not ready to be in this bed without James, at least not yet. Where am I going to sleep tonight? I'm not sleeping in the bed where Anthony and Cindy slept, and I'm too scared to sleep on the couch next to the hall after the night Cindy appeared. I got up and walked out of the bedroom, closing the door behind me.

I slowly opened the door to Willow's room. She was sleeping so peacefully. There is a night light giving off a soft glow and lighting up the room. It's the only place in the house that didn't scare me or make me feel emotional. I crept over to her bed and curled up next to her, trying not to wake her. For the first time today, I didn't feel uneasy or scared. I'm not sure why it felt comforting being next to her. Maybe it's because I wasn't alone. I fell asleep and slept through the night.

After an uninterrupted night of good sleep, I stretched and let out a yawn. Once I opened my eyes, I screamed and jumped so hard I fell onto the floor. I quickly scurried across the room and leaned my back up against the wall. When I opened my eyes, I thought Cindy was in front of me, staring at me. For a minute, I forgot where I was, and soon realized it was Willow.

"Auntie, are you okay?"

"Yes, I'm sorry. I got scared for a minute." I stuttered, still terrified and trying to pull myself together. "You look just like... um... you look... like someone else."

She sat up in her bed. "Daddy says I look just like mommy."

I didn't know how to respond to her. I picked myself up off the floor, still feeling terrified and weak in the knees.

"Auntie Vicky, why did you sleep in here last night? Were you scared?"

I turned toward the door. "I'm having a hard time adjusting, that's all. Why don't you get ready for the day while I go cook us breakfast."

"Okay," she said.

Something as simple as spending time in the kitchen to cook breakfast was challenging for me. When I reached for a glass, paranoia set in and I had to look over my shoulder to make sure there wasn't anyone standing behind me, ready to reach out and grab me. I had to move the glasses to a different cabinet. If I'm going to be staying here, there needs to be some changes. It's a good day to go to town and do some shopping. This place needs a make-over, starting with nightlights in every room and both hallways.

I yelled across the house, "Willow, breakfast is done!" I didn't get a response, so I went to her room. "Willow," I said as I opened her door. She is sitting on the edge of her bed, eyes wide open, and staring out into nothing. What is she doing? What? Not her too? Her mother did the same thing. This can't be happening. "Willow." Still no response. I clapped my hands together in front of her face and yelled, "Willow!"

"Yes, auntie?"

"There you are. Are you feeling okay?"

She didn't move a muscle. "Yes, why?"

"I've been calling you for breakfast and you sat here ignoring me."

"I'm so sorry, auntie. I didn't hear you."

"Willow, how often does this happen to you?"

She sat there like a statue. "What do you mean?"

"Oh, nevermind, go eat your breakfast."

"Okay," she said. Then she got up and walked out of the room.

While she sat and ate, I went and got ready for the day.

"Willow, how about you and I go shopping together in town today?" I said, while I sat down across from her at the table.

She looked up at me and paused for a moment. "Your lipstick is very pretty, Auntie Vicky."

"Thank you, Willow."

"It looks just like my lipstick," she said.

I asked her, "Do you have this color lipstick also?"

"Yes, I will show you." She got up and went to her room for a minute. When she came back, she handed it to me.

"Where did you get this? Did you steal this from me?"

"No," she said.

I got annoyed, and raised my voice. "Don't lie to me. Did you take this from my purse?"

She stood there, calm, with no emotion. "No, I didn't get it from you."

I stood up and grabbed my purse from the counter. I opened it and there it was, the same lipstick sitting inside. It's the only lipstick I buy. Where did she get this? Maybe I left it behind in James's room one night?

I asked her, "Willow, where did you get this lipstick?"

She looked up at me, almost looking like she was going to cry, and said, "It was on the ground in front of the barn the day daddy disappeared."

Her statement almost floored me. I started feeling weak and had to sit back down in the chair. I remembered having to pick up my purse after it got pulled from my hand. I never found my lipstick after that day. It must have fallen out. How could I be so stupid and miss it lying on the ground?

"Willow, did you tell anyone you found this?"

She reached out and snatched it from my hand. "No, I never told anyone I found it."

"Good, make sure you tell no one about this because you are too young to be wearing make-up," I said, lying to her.

"Auntie?"

"Yes, Willow?"

"How did you get the big scar on your neck?"

I adjusted my scarf, not realizing my scar was showing. "I really don't want to talk about it. Come on, let's go shopping."

She got up from her chair and stepped over to me. She placed her hand on my shoulder, leaned into my ear, and whispered. "It's okay, auntie, I know how you got the scar on your neck." Then she walked out the front door and got into the car.

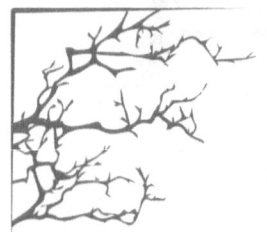

Chapter 30

Shopping was exhausting, especially after the morning I had. I bought enough groceries to feed a small army, new curtains, and every night light they had in the store. I spent the rest of the day cleaning up the house and re-organizing to make the place look different so I could feel a little less creeped out and frightened about being here.

Willow spent most of her time sitting out in the backyard. She didn't move for most of the day. She just sat there like a statue. There is something eerie and sinister about her. I better tell her it's time to come in. I yelled out the back door. "Willow!" I got no response. Where is she? She was out here a few minutes ago. "Willow, where are you?" I yelled.

I couldn't find her anywhere outside. Is she in the barn? There's no way she is in there. She doesn't like the barn as much as I don't. I kept calling out for her as I made my way over to check inside.

One door was slightly opened. I stepped inside and felt sick to my stomach. I flipped the light switch, and the lights didn't come on. It was dark and musty inside. I called out, "Willow." Still no answer. I walked as slow as I could past the stalls, looking in every direction, hoping no one was waiting to jump out at me. As soon as I reached the stall where Cindy bound James and I to the wall, I trembled with fear and got sick. After I threw up all over the floor, I glanced over at the stairs leading up to the hayloft. I wonder if she is hiding up there?

"Willow! This isn't funny. Please answer me," I begged. I pushed myself to go up the stairs in search of her. It was dark and dusty. I could barely see, so I opened the door at the end of the loft to let some light in. I stood there looking over the backyard, continuing to call out for her. Then I heard footsteps coming up the stairs, one step at a time, in a slow, methodical fashion. Clomp. Clomp. Clomp. "Willow, is that you?" Still, no response. I started to panic. Then I saw her blonde hair as she approached the top step.

"Willow, why would you not answer me? I've been calling out to you."

Still, she gave no response. She stood there, in her dress, with her hand behind her back, hiding something. She kept staring in my direction, expressionless. Then she walked toward me. As she approached me, she didn't stop. I backed up as far as I could go without falling from the barn while she continued pushing toward me. "Willow, stop! You're going to knock me out of the barn. A fall from this height would kill me!"

Then she looked up and spoke. "I have something for you."

I got nervous about what she might be hiding behind her back. I shivered. "What do you have?"

She pulled her arm around to show me. "I picked you a flower. It's mommy's favorite."

As soon as I saw her holding a daisy, I almost fainted and fell out the door. It's the same flower her mother placed in my hair on the night she tried to kill me. I got stricken with fear, so I took off running back down the stairs, out of the barn and into the house.

I laid on James's bed, crying. How does she know about the flower? Maybe Anthony told her daisies are her mom's favorite? A few minutes later, I heard Willow's bedroom door shut and then I fell asleep.

The following day, Willow had her therapy and meetings with her counselors. It takes most of the day up, so I dropped her off. I went back to the house to finish rearranging things and clean up James's bedroom so I could start staying in there. I cleaned up, changed out the curtains and placed night lights into every electrical socket in the house. I even got a dim bulb for the lamp in the living room so it can always stay lit.

I went into Willow's bedroom to make up her bed. There isn't much in her room. Besides the bed, there is a dresser and a wooden toy box. There were princess figurines on top of her dresser, neatly placed and untouched. Her dresser drawers were full of clothing and nothing more. The toy box has dolls and games neatly stacked inside. It doesn't seem like she plays with any of her stuff. Maybe she is a neat freak? What does she do all day in this room? I made her bed, making sure it was as neat as the rest of her room. When I started tucking the sheet under the mattress, I felt something. I reached under and pulled out an envelope. It's addressed to Willow. The return address is from the psychiatric hospital. It's a letter from Cindy.

I hurried to make the bed and went to sit on the couch to read it.

Dear Willow,

I am writing this letter to you because I don't know how long it will be before I can see you. Right now, you are inside of mommy's belly, kicking me like crazy. You like to keep mommy up most nights, kicking. I don't mind it though. I just lie here, holding my belly and telling you stories all night until you calm down. I imagine what you're going to look like after you are born. Will you look like daddy or will you look like mommy? Will you have dark hair or light blonde hair? No matter who you look like, I know you will be the most beautiful thing to ever exist. I wish you could stay in mommy's belly forever. I know once you're born, they will take you from me because of where I am. I hope daddy hurries up and gets you as soon as he can. I know he will love you and take care of you. Your dad is a good man and I love him very much. Sooner or later, we will finally meet. Once daddy gets custody of you, he will bring you to visit me. I can't wait to hold you in my arms and kiss you.

I wish it didn't have to be this way, but mommy did something to some bad people, who were trying to hurt daddy and I. I had to do it to keep us safe. I hope someday you understand.

I want you to know how much I love you. Carrying you around in my belly with me every day brings me so much joy. We haven't met yet and I already love you more than life. No matter what happens, I will always love you. One day, you, daddy and I will be together. Until we meet. Love, Mommy.

I thought to myself, at least you gave birth to your daughter, Cindy! You took my child away from me and soon I will take away your child. I wonder what time it is? "Shit," I said. I'm going to be late picking up Willow. I threw the letter in my purse and ran out the door to go get her.

I barely made it there on time. The car ride back was the same as always. I tried to talk to her, and she ignored me the entire way home. There is something seriously wrong with this girl. I'm not convinced therapy is helping her.

Willow is now in bed for the night and I can finally relax in bed myself. It felt much better to be back in James's room now that it was clean and back in order. I am still heartbroken and I know it will never go away, but it is comforting to be back in his bed, even though he is no longer here. Sometimes I go to his grave to visit him, and no matter how much I rehearse in my head what I'm going to say to him, the only words I can seem to get out are "I love you" before I start crying.

I slid into bed, shut off the lamp, and fell asleep. It didn't take long before I began to wake up and feel restless. It must be the middle of the night. It was still dark. I am thirsty and in need of some water. I refuse to go out to the kitchen. I now get it from the bathroom sink. As soon as I turned the lamp on, I screamed when I saw someone standing at the end of the bed.

"Ah! Willow, how long have you been standing there for? You almost gave me a heart attack!"

She tilted her head down, put her fists in a ball and in an angry tone screamed, "Where is it, Vicky?"

I asked, "Where is what?"

She clenched her jaw and spoke through her teeth. "You know exactly what I'm talking about! Where is my letter from mommy? What did you do with it?"

"Willow, I'm so sorry. I was making your bed, and it fell on the floor. I meant to give it to you when I picked you up, but I must have forgotten. It's in my purse on the counter."

She glared at me, while thinking about what I just said to her. "Don't you ever touch my stuff again or you will be sorry!" Then she stomped out of the room and down to the kitchen. After a minute, I heard her stomp back to her room and slam the door shut.

I couldn't believe the way she spoke to me. She definitely has some anger issues. I wonder how long she stood at the foot of the bed for? It's kind of chilling and weird that she would stand there in the dark, watching me sleep. I got up and locked the door before getting back into bed.

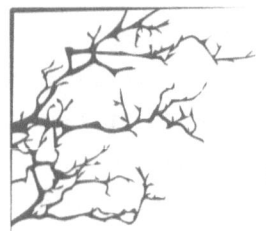

Chapter 31

The following morning, as I walked past Willow's bedroom door, I could hear her talking to someone. I pressed my ear against her door to listen in. "Okay. Yes, I know. I love you too," she said. I opened the door and found her sitting on her bed. I glanced around the room, confused. "Willow, who were you talking to?"

She turned her head toward me and said, "No one."

Why is she lying to me? She could have told me she was talking to herself, but she chose to lie. I am starting to get really annoyed with this girl. "Get ready and come have breakfast," I said.

She got up from her bed without saying another word.

We both sat at the table eating breakfast. Willow kept turning her head and looking up. It annoyed the hell out of me. I really need to get rid of this girl before she drives me crazy. "Willow, what are you looking at?"

Then she looked directly into my eyes and said, "Mommy says you're a bad person."

I almost choked at her response. "Your mommy?" I asked.

She looked up again over her shoulder and said, "Yes, mommy told me you're an evil person."

I felt faint. What is wrong with this girl?

Then she turned her eyes up at me and giggled.

"Willow, do you think this is funny? This is not funny at all."

"I'm sorry, Auntie Vicky. I was laughing at what mommy told me last night. She said we should tie you in the barn stall and leave you there forever."

I jumped up and ran over to the kitchen sink, where I got sick. How does she know about Cindy tying me up in the stall? This is all completely crazy. I'm losing it with this girl. I walked back over to the table and snapped at her. "I will show you exactly what I'm going to do to the barn. Go get in the car!"

She picked up her head and said, "No, I don't like you."

I lost my patience with her, so I grabbed her by the hair, dragging her out of her chair while she screamed in pain. I leaned down and got right in her face, gripping her hair tighter, and pulling her head back. "You don't have to like me, little girl, but you do have to listen to me. Now, go get in the fucking car!"

She folded her arms and looked at me like she wanted to kill me. Then she stomped out of the house and got into the car.

I parked on the street, outside of the hardware store. "Willow, stay in the car and don't move. I will be back in a minute." She sat there with her arms still folded, acting like I didn't exist.

After I got what I needed from the store, I went back to the car. Where the hell is the little brat? I told her to stay in the car. I swear I'm going to strangle her when we get back to the house. I noticed her out of the corner of my eye. She was standing further down the sidewalk with a woman and pointing in my direction. I stomped over to her, and as I got close, the woman yelled out to me. "Stop right there and don't come any closer. This precious child told me you forced her into the car and took her. You can't just kidnap children and get away with it. The police are on their way right now."

I could feel my face getting red with anger. Willow stood there, next to the woman, grinning at me while she had her arms folded in front of her. My eyes pierced her. I need to get rid of this girl and send her back to her mommy and daddy once and for all.

A police car pulled up and parked next to her and the woman. I watched as a cop got out of the car and walked over to her. The woman started yelling as soon as the policeman approached her. "Her, right there." She pointed directly at me. "She forced this beautiful girl into her car and tried to kidnap her."

The cop looked at me with a puzzled look as I shrugged my shoulders. He was one of the policemen there the day they found me lying in the box, almost dead. "Ma'am, I know who this woman is. This is Vicky, and this is her adopted daughter, Willow. I will take it from here."

She took her arm off of Willow and walked away disgusted and embarrassed by what she was just put through. "Shame on you," she said to Willow as she walked away.

He put his hand on my shoulder. "It will get easier, Vicky. I know it doesn't seem like it, but it will. The both of you have been through a lot, and it's going to take some time to heal. If you need anything, reach out to me," he said.

"Thank you, I appreciate it," I said.

Then he turned his attention to Willow. "I know how difficult it has been for you. Try to get along with Vicky. She is only trying to help." Then he gave a smile, got into his car and drove off.

"Willow, get in the car, now," I said, still upset and annoyed at the stunt she just pulled.

Once we got home, I began installing the locks I purchased onto the barn doors. I wanted to make sure no one would ever go into the barn again. When I was almost finished, I heard the back door of the house slam shut. Willow came marching over to me. She stopped and stiffened her posture.

"Willow, do you need something?"

She took a long look at me and asked, "Did you try to kill my daddy?"

I stood here, confused and wondering why she would ask me such a question. "What? Why would you ask me such a thing?"

"I've been talking to mommy, and she said you tried to kill daddy."

I leaned down, "Your mommy is dead, you little brat. Your father told me she died giving birth to you. You're the one who killed your precious mommy!"

Once she heard what I said, she slapped me across the face and spit on me. I grabbed her by the wrist and pulled her into the barn, dragging her up the stairs while she fought and screamed the whole way. I brought her over to the door, shoving her into the opening.

"You want to know how your daddy died? I will show you!" I held her wrist and hung her part way out of the opening, watching her dangle.

She started pleading with me to pull her back in. "I'm so sorry, Auntie Vicky. I didn't mean to upset you."

"Willow, you need to understand something. Your mother is dead. I don't want to hear anymore about it."

She focused her gaze beside me and said in a soft voice, "Don't look, she is standing behind you right now."

My knees got weak, and I froze in fear. I pulled her back in and turned around to see if Cindy was really there. A sharp pain in the back of my leg buckled me to the floor. As I kneeled on the floor, holding my leg, I realized the pain was from Willow kicking me before she ran out of the barn.

Ugh! This brat is really getting on my nerves. I should have dropped her to her death and put her out in the woods like I did to her father. I finished installing the locks on the barn. "There, now no one is getting back inside, especially the little brat."

I limped my way back into the house to make dinner. The sooner I feed the little bitch, the sooner I can put her in bed so I can relax. In the process of making dinner I opened the drawer to get the kitchen knife. What? Where is it? I checked all the other drawers and still didn't find it.

I went in search of Willow. I found her outback coming out of the woods. "Willow, get over here. Now!" As she got close to me I reached down and grabbed her by the wrist to drag her into the house. She immediately pulled her arm back and waved her finger at me. Then she spoke in a soft voice. "I wouldn't do that if I were you. She is watching you and you don't want to make her mad."

"Who is watching me?"

"Mommy is watching you. She has been watching you a lot and she doesn't like the way you've been treating me."

I reached down and grabbed her by her wrist again and started dragging her into the house. "You better listen to me you little brat. You are to stay out of those woods. I better not find out you're out there again. The woods are off limits and I mean it. Do you understand me?"

"Yes, auntie."

"Good, now get over here and look in this drawer. Can you tell me what's missing?"

"No, auntie. What's missing?"

"The knife is missing. Did you take it Willow?"

"No, auntie."

"Do not lie to me or you will be sorry. The knife didn't get up and walk away on its own. Tell me where it is and you won't be in trouble."

"I don't know where it is. Maybe mommy took it."

"Of course you would say that Willow. Did your dead mommy come into the house and take the knife? Let me guess, she plans on killing me with it? Am I right, you little brat? Is your dead mommy going to kill me?"

She looked up at me, staring.

"Come on, spit it out! Is your dead fucking mommy going to kill me with the knife that disappeared from the kitchen? The knife I'm sure you took!"

"No, auntie, not yet. She is waiting for daddy to get here."

"Ugh! I have had enough of you Willow! Get out of my sight before I do something I regret. You can go to bed hungry. Go to your room for the night. You can cry to your dead parents for all I care. I don't want to see you until morning."

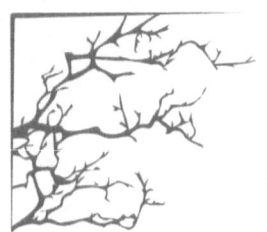

Chapter 32

The next few days were uneventful. Willow pretty much kept to herself. I understand why she is avoiding me. I did threaten to drop her to her death. I am still shocked by how unafraid she seemed. Yes, she pleaded with me not to drop her, but she acted pretty calm for someone who was about to die. Her spells are getting worse and more frequent. She has been spacing out quite a bit the last few days. I wish I could say I'm not concerned, but I am. I never know what to expect from her. After her outbursts, anything is possible, and her imaginary relationship with her dead mother? What is that all about? It's kind of disturbing. Her mother had an imaginary friend growing up, but a dead mother? Something is seriously wrong with this girl.

If I didn't miss James so much, I would blame him. He should have taken care of Cindy and Anthony when I told him to. Now, I can only dream about what my life would be like if he did what I asked him to do. Gosh, I miss him. He would come to see me every night after work for a few hours. I would always have dinner ready for him when he got there. I miss all the nights he would stay over. We got a kick out of his 'work trips'. He would lie and tell Cindy he had to leave for a couple of weeks and then spend those weeks with me. Sometimes we would leave and actually go on vacation trips together. I really miss him.

It took me a while to get over him marrying Cindy. It wasn't his fault. He wanted to marry me. The poor guy actually proposed to me and I turned him down. I felt horrible about it. He drifted away for a few months and refused to talk to me, but he couldn't stay away forever. He loved me too much. I honestly believe he married Cindy just to teach me a lesson, and it worked. As soon as he married her, I wanted him even more. I didn't want to share him with anyone else.

I always told Cindy I was seeing guys from the health club, but the truth is, I was seeing James behind her back. She always asked me when I was going to settle down and get married, and I told her I didn't want to. Honestly, it was because I couldn't get married. She was married to the man I wanted to be with.

The day Cindy told me about Anthony made me so happy. I got a glimpse of hope that I would get James back for good, but all Cindy and Anthony seemed to do was get in the way of us being together. It made me sick pretending to be Cindy's friend all those years so I could sleep with her husband behind her back. I should have killed her myself, long ago.

I remember the day James and I found this house. We both loved it so much, he bought it. He proposed to me on the porch the day he closed on the loan. It devastated him when I told him I wasn't ready to get married. Now that I'm back in our home, it doesn't feel the same. It's terrifying to be in this house after everything that's happened here and it's lonely without him. Once I'm done killing Willow, I plan on leaving and never looking back. Maybe I will sell my health clubs and spend the rest of my life living on a beach somewhere.

I wondered where Willow was and what she was up to. I haven't seen her much today. I went outside looking for her and couldn't find her. When I went back into the house, I found her standing in the living room. She wasn't doing anything, just standing there. Her eyes are locked on me. I snarled at her, "What are you looking at?"

She continued staring at me and said, "Mommy and daddy said you need to die."

I'm losing my patience with this girl. I snapped at her, "Your mommy is dead, just like your daddy, you little brat! I don't have time for your bullshit."

She crossed her arms and stomped her foot on the floor. "It's not bullshit, auntie!"

I almost reached out my arms to grab her by the throat. I wanted to choke her to death, but I restrained myself. "Willow, do not swear at me," I said in a calm voice.

"Auntie, you refuse to listen to me. Mommy said she is going to kill you once and for all."

I leaned down and got right in her face while placing my hands on her shoulders. "Willow, I know how hard it must be for you to lose both of your parents, but you need to get over it. They are gone and they're never coming back. You need to let it go. I don't want to keep hearing about it everyday. You're beginning to drive me nuts."

Then I noticed a police car pull up to the house. I looked right at her and asked, "What the hell did you do now? I'm getting really tired of your games."

She put her head down and said, "I didn't do anything, auntie, I swear."

"Fine, go to your room while I see what they want." I thought, "Such a strange girl. I can't wait to kill her so she can be with her mommy and daddy for good."

I walked out onto the porch to greet the policeman and find out what was going on. I was relieved to see it was Ethan. "Hi Ethan, what brings you here today?" I asked.

He took his hat off while he walked toward me. The look on his face was concerning. I thought, what now? What did the little brat do this time?

Ethan stopped in front of me and began to speak. "I have some very concerning news, Vicky. I don't know why the hospital didn't report it weeks ago, but Cindy escaped. We are trying to find her."

I collapsed. Ethan grabbed me as I fell and helped me sit down on the steps. "You're lying to me, Ethan. There is no way she escaped. She is dead. She died while giving birth to Willow. This can't be right."

He looked at me funny and asked, "Who told you Cindy died?"

"Anthony told me," I said.

Ethan looked even more puzzled. "Listen, Vicky, you need to take this seriously. Have you seen Cindy at all? We need to find her as soon as possible."

I sat here in shock at what he just said to me. Why would Anthony lie about Cindy dying? "No, I haven't seen her. Ethan, I have to go." I picked myself up off of the porch and ran into the house, slamming the door behind me and locking it. I ran around the house, locking all the windows and doors. This can't be happening. I began to cry as I watched Ethan drive away.

Guns. James had guns. I wonder if they are still here. I went to his bedroom and started tearing everything apart. I pulled out all of his drawers, throwing them onto the floor. I ripped everything off of the shelves in the closet. I checked the entire room and found nothing. I tore apart the closet in the hall and found nothing there either. Maybe they are in Anthony's room?

I ran to Anthony's room and started tearing it apart. I didn't find any guns. The last place to check is his closet. I pulled everything out of the closet and didn't find any guns there, either. I reached up on the shelf and accidentally knocked down a bunch of envelopes. What I saw sent chills up my spine. I picked them up. They are letters addressed to Willow, from Cindy. The date stamps on them span from the time she was locked up until recently. This can't be right. I opened up one of the envelopes. It's empty. The letter is missing. I checked the rest, and they were all empty.

I stormed out of the room and barged into Willow's room, where she was sitting on her bed. I tore out her drawers, emptying them onto the floor. I flipped over her toy box. She yelled at me, "What are you doing? I told you to never touch my stuff!"

I leaned over the bed and grabbed her by the shirt. "Where are they, Willow?"

"Where is what?" she asked.

I tightened my grip. "You know exactly what I'm talking about. The letters from your mom. Where are the letters, you little brat?"

"Auntie, I don't know what you're talking about."

I pulled her closer. "Now is not the time. Don't play dumb with me." Then I thought about what Willow said to me when

I was putting the locks on the barn. "Did you try to kill my daddy?" I felt like I was going to pass out from fear. No, this can't be. He has to be dead. There is no way he survived a fall like that.

I ran out the back door and kept running until I found the spot in the woods where I laid Anthony's body. Where is it? How can it be gone? This is right where I left him. I got frantic and started looking everywhere. There is no trace of him or his skeleton. What the hell is going on? I started sobbing. "Pull yourself together," I said. I need to get Willow and leave. It's not safe here for me anymore.

I walked through the back door of the house, closing it behind me. When I looked up, I fell to the floor in terror. "Hello, Vicky," Cindy said, grimacing at me. The three of them were standing side by side, holding hands. Cindy was also holding a knife, just like the one she cut me with years ago.

I stuttered in fear, "You... you are supposed to be dead, Cindy. Anthony told me you died in childbirth. How are you still alive?"

Anthony looked down at me with a smile on his face and said, "I lied."

I cried harder. "Anthony, you are supposed to be dead, too."

He stared at me briefly, still smiling. "It took a while to recover from my injuries, now here I am."

"Baby," Cindy said, turning toward Anthony.

"Yes, love?"

"Will you please take Willow outside? I have some unfinished business with our dear friend Vicky."

"Sure, baby," he said. Then he picked up Willow and walked out the front door with her.

Anthony put his hands over Willow's ears while loud screams shrieked from inside of the house. After a couple of minutes, it got quiet, and Cindy came walking out with blood on her hands. She looked up at Anthony. "It's now finished. Can you do something for me?"

Anthony said, "Sure, baby, anything for you. What do you need?"

Cindy paused briefly, taking one last look at her home before turning to Anthony.

"Burn it to the ground."

The End